A CHRISTMAS BRIDE FOR THE HIDDEN HERO

THE MAIL ORDER BRIDES OF GRAY ROCK

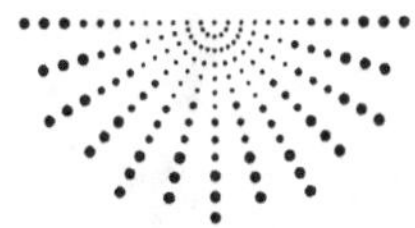

INDIANA WAKE

A CHRISTMAS BRIDE FOR THE HIDDEN HERO

Welcome to this series of western historical romances. This is a new series that I have been working on for some time and I can't wait to share the books with you.

All of them are a complete romance and a full story. They are also sweet and clean with no nasty surprises.

Carrie McCord was worried about her son. He had a good job and is a lovely man but there were no women in the mining town and Jamison didn't seem to be interested in finding a wife.

Hoping for grandchildren before she was too old to enjoy them, Carrie took things into her own hands and sent off for a mail order bride. Read all about it in The Miner's Courageous Bride.

Now that her son is married, other miners are looking for brides. Can Carrie work her magic once more?

Find more books in this series here

Find out about new releases, get special offers, and receive 3 free books by joining my exclusive newsletter

CHAPTER ONE

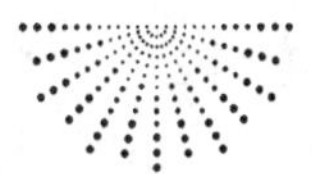

"So, the rumors are true? You're matchmaking again, Mrs. McCord?"

Christmas was only two months away. It was Carrie Hill's favorite time of the year, hence, she obsessed about it even though they hadn't even celebrated Thanksgiving. There was no particular reason for this. Carrie was just always unusually excited during this time of the year. It was the season of love, togetherness, good food, family, laughter, and happy tears... it was Christmas. The season never failed to remind her of the things, and people she was grateful for in her life.

For the first time, in a long time, Carrie was going to celebrate her favorite season as a happily married woman. The mere thought of it thrilled her. She had only been married to the local sheriff, Carl for a couple of months, but she felt like the happiest woman on Earth.

"Yes, Zachary," Carrie answered. "Don't forget it's Mrs. Hill now. How can I help you today?"

Carl was mostly to blame for Carrie's change of heart. At first, when it seemed very unlikely that he was going to forgive her for her deceit, she had completely given up on matchmaking. Carrie had believed that she had failed. She believed she was unfit to be making matches. If she couldn't make a match work for herself, and since she had failed to make accurate matches in the past, then there was every possibility that she was terrible at matchmaking.

However, thanks to the reassurance from her family and some very successful matches, Carrie found a reason to start again. The town needed her, and she was happy to be of help. Plus, making these matches was thrilling for Carrie. It gave her life meaning. She was back in business, and as always, she had people waiting for her magic. People like Zachary.

"You have no idea how happy I am to hear this," Zachary beamed. "I think I'm ready, Mrs. McCord. I'm ready to settle down."

Carrie tilted her head to the side. "You think? So, you're not sure?"

"No, I'm sure. I'm ready," Zachary stuttered. "I'm just a bit nervous. Please find me a wife, Mrs. McCord. Or... sorry, it's Mrs. Hill now? You know... you just told me but I forgot and I know you're married to the sheriff."

Carrie smiled. "Just called me Carrie, Zachary."

"All right." He nodded. "And you can call me Zack. Short for Zachary."

"I see." She chuckled.

For some strange reason, Carrie had mixed feelings about Zachary Warner. He was young, and also a miner like Jamison, but he wasn't as... neat, and neither did he look friendly. Or at least he didn't appear to be. His shoulder-length brown hair was uncombed and dull, his clothes were rumpled, he had an unkempt dark beard, and his boot had a hole in it. The man also had a big build. Tall, broad shoulders and a fierce gaze. It was evident that Zachary didn't pay much attention to his looks, and Carrie was finding it difficult not to judge him for it.

But on the brighter side, he seemed nice. He had a warm smile too, and he seemed genuine. Carrie was one to always trust her gut, and follow her instincts, but looking at Zachary, she didn't know whether she could make him into good husband material.

"Carrie, I can assure you, my intentions are good," he said, breaking the awkward silence.

"Come and sit, Zach," Carrie answered. "And tell me why you think you want a wife."

"No, I don't think. I know I want a wife," he replied and took his seat on the bench outside Carrie's home. "I've been alone for way too long. I see what you do for the other miners, for yourself, for the sheriff. I want that too. I want a good family, a wife, and kids... I want love. You've been married for a while now..."

"Yes?"

"Doesn't it feel nice?"

Carrie chuckled and shook her head. "It does. It really does."

"Well, there you have it. I want that too. I promised my mother I'd start a family of my own before she passed away."

Carrie crossed her arms. "How old are you, Zach?"

"I turned twenty-four last month," he answered. "Why? Do you think I'm not ready for the responsibility? Because I think I am. You have to trust me, Carrie. All I seek is a better life for myself."

"I don't doubt that. Everyone wants a better life for themselves. I believe everyone needs someone by their side to help them through this journey called life. Doing it alone can be a bit boring sometimes. I can say this from experience. Plus, it's the whole reason I started match-making in the first place."

Zachary sighed in relief. "So, you'll help me?"

Carrie clicked her tongue. "I'm not sure, Zach. I would have to think about it."

"Oh, Carrie," he said with a sigh. "What's the issue? If you tell me what I need to do, I'll do it. I truly want this for myself."

"I know…"

It didn't feel like it was her place to mention his appearance. At least not until she was certain she could get him a bride. Zachary reminded Carrie of Wyatt. How rough he looked when he first came to her and how she had ignored all the bad signs and helped him. If she learned anything from Wyatt's case, it was that appearances weren't everything. In the end, what really mattered was how the person felt. How the person treated others and their plans for the future.

Although Zachary didn't look like a man willing to start a family, he sounded like one. There was desperation in his eyes, and judging by the number of times that he had visited her, even when she was unsure she was going to continue matchmaking, Carrie believed his intentions were pure.

"Let's see how it goes," she told him. "I will draft a letter for the advert and send it to the newspaper. Hopefully, we will get a response from a sweet lady willing to travel west. But you should know that these things take time, Zach. Usually, letters take about ten days to reach the East, and it might take from a month to six months before someone decides to write back. We can't tell. But you know me. I'm not the type that gives up easily. There is someone out there for you, and we'll find them."

"It would be a miracle if I can find a match by Christmas, wouldn't it?" he asked. "I know I'm a bit rough around the edges and I don't look like a fine man, but I was hoping that I wouldn't have to spend the holiday alone again. I have a sister. Her name is Peggy. I helped her a great deal when she got married. She lives in California now with her husband and she always writes to me. She's happy. Christmas is my favorite season. There's a particular feeling that accompanies the season and it always makes me so happy. But when I lie in bed at the end of the day, alone, it gets depressing. I mean, it's the season of love, isn't it? I should be surrounded by love on a day like that."

"It is." Carrie smiled and patted him on the back. "Be optimistic, Zach. One thing I have learned in the last two years is that what is yours will always find you. Always. No matter how far away it is. Everything we experience in our life is all part of God's big plan. It doesn't matter when it happens. What matters is that you're happy when it does. Keep your head up."

"I will."

Carrie asked him a lot of questions about what he wanted, what he liked to do, and what sort of woman he was after. A lot of what she did was on feelings but her questions got to the bottom of things for her.

"Did I get them right?" he asked as she closed her book.

"There's no right answer. Don't worry, I'll let you know if anything comes up."

"I'll be grateful," he said, rising to his feet. "Thank you so much, Carrie. I'm glad you're back."

"I am too," she answered. "Have a nice day at work, Zach. Say hello to Jamie for me if you see him."

"I'll make sure I do. Have a nice day too. I'll visit some other time."

Carrie waved him goodbye then sat back down on the bench and sighed. She truly was glad to be back, but Zachary's case seemed like it was going to be a tough shell to crack. Carrie was not one to run from a challenge, but she couldn't help but wonder if she was going to be successful with his case like she had been with Wyatt.

This is different...

Wyatt's case wasn't the same. Unlike Wyatt, Zach had a fair-paying job, and he wasn't an outcast. He had better odds, and since she was successful in finding Wyatt a bride, she could do the same for Zach. It was going to be tasking, but she was willing to give it her all.

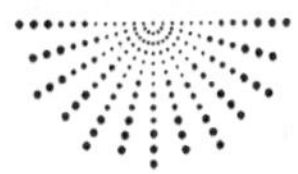

arrie crumpled up a piece of paper and threw it on the table. She sighed, staring at all the balls of paper littering the table and floor. All the efforts that she had wasted. It was difficult to craft a letter for the advert when she was still on the fence about helping Zach whether to find a bride or not. Carrie wanted to only concentrate on the good he had to offer, but she found herself doubting his ability to actually take care of his bride. The more she thought about it, the more she questioned everything.

"What is it?" Carl asked, leaning on the table. He had just gotten back from the sheriff's office and had not even put away his gun.

"Nothing," she answered, shaking her head. "How was work today? Did anything interesting happen?"

"No, and don't change the subject. You look stressed and apparently frustrated by something," he answered. "Tell me what the problem is and we'll fix it together. Like we always do."

Carrie emitted another sigh. "So, as we discussed, I've decided to continue matchmaking. I realize that it brings me so much joy to help people come together, and I want that in my life. I agreed to meet with Zachary Warner, one of the miners this morning."

"All right," he said, nodding. "I guess you weren't impressed?"

"By his looks, no... but he seems like a good person. I'm sure under the unkempt hair, and raggedy clothes is a handsome young man. I mean, he has beautiful brown eyes and an equally engaging smile. However, if he is comfortable looking like that every day, then that means he doesn't take himself seriously!"

Carl pulled out a chair and sat by her side. "My love, miners are busy men who work underground in horrible and dirty situations. It shouldn't be a surprise that he looks... unkempt. Not that I'm justifying it, but he probably doesn't see the need to wash that often because he's only going back in the ground again tomorrow. You know how men can be."

"I know, but that's not a valid reason not to pay attention to your appearance. I don't doubt that Zach is a sweet person, but I'm caught at a crossroads. Should I mention this in the advert or just leave it?"

"Carrie." Carl chuckled. "It's not something that cannot be fixed. I mean, you did the same for Wyatt. You practically changed his life as well as his appearance."

"That was different," she insisted. "With Wyatt, I was helping a kid who had nothing. Zach is a miner. It's a job, but I can tell that he's struggling a bit. It feels like he can only take care of himself, not a family. He has quite an intimidating build, and to be honest, I can't just ask him to cut his hair, get new clothes and change his appearance. He might find it insulting."

"Sure, you can. But don't you think that's not the issue at hand? We need to find him a bride first. That is the first step in motivating him. He might be a hard sell because he doesn't look like the romantic type. I think that Zachary hasn't been paying any attention to his appearance because he has no one to impress. He's a miner, surely he can change his looks, but he just doesn't see the need to. Once you give him a reason, he won't hesitate to clean up and act accordingly."

Carrie turned to him. "Do you think so?"

"I know so," he answered, embracing her. "You can work your magic on anyone. After all, your tricks worked wonders with us. I'm sure it'll have the same effect on Zach. Is his appearance the only thing that you're skeptical about?"

"It's the major thing, there are other reasons too. I mean, I know Zach, but not like I know the other matches I've made. What if he isn't as nice as I think he is, or what if his match finds him a bit intimidating?"

"What do you personally think of him?"

Carrie paused to think. "Well, he's hardworking, that's one thing. He's almost always at the mine, even though he doesn't make that much money there like the others. He's sweet, and he knows how to communicate what he's thinking. Unlike Jamison, I don't think he keeps his emotions bottled up. He seems like the kind that would do his best to make any bride happy. When I say his best, I mean he seems like the type that would go to lengths for someone he cares about."

"Good. All you have to do, is focus on these qualities, and you have yourself an advert," he told her. "I think Zachary is hardworking and nice too. He'd make any bride happy."

Carrie nodded and sighed.

"What's your gut telling you?" he asked.

"I'm not sure. I do have doubts, but I really want to send the advert too," she replied. "That means my gut is telling me to go for it, isn't it? It's similar to the feeling I had when Wyatt first came to me."

"And remind me, how did things turn out with Wyatt?"

"Well, apart from the fact that you almost jailed him for life, I'd say things turned out pretty good."

Carl chuckled and shook his head. "I was just doing my job. Plus, at least now, we know that Wyatt has good intentions. He's doing better than I imagined he would; he's happy too. All thanks to my wife. You know, this is the first Christmas we'd be spending together as a married couple?"

Carrie lifted her head and pecked him on the cheek. "I know. I look forward to it."

Hearing Carl's words reminded Carrie of Zachary's wish. He wanted to spend Christmas with someone, rather than be alone like he had done in the previous years. While Carrie was doubtful that she could make that happen, she at least wanted to give him some good news that would comfort him during the Christmas season. It would be a great feat if she at least found him a nice lady to correspond with during the holiday.

"Are you hungry?" she asked. "Your dinner is on the table. Why don't you put that gun in the cupboard and eat before you go to bed? You look tired."

"I am tired," he said and placed a peck on her forehead. "Thank you. I'll be right back. I can read the advert before you send it."

"Yes." She nodded. "Thank you for the help. You really put everything into perspective."

"I'm only glad I can help."

As Carl retreated to the room, Carrie sat up and put her pen on the paper. Like Carl had suggested, she figured it was best to focus on the good attributes that Zachary had to offer. Thankfully, they outweighed the negative.

Getting the advert into the paper wasn't the problem. All Carrie hoped was that it got to the right woman. Someone that would like Zachary the way he wanted to be loved, and someone deserving of his love and kindness.

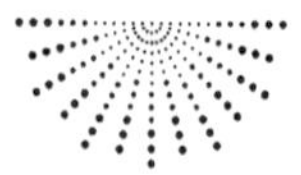

CHAPTER THREE

"Uncle, I will not marry him. I don't want to. I've been telling you, but you don't want to listen to me."

Mabel Mason crossed her arms in an attempt to look serious. She couldn't count how many times she had had this discussion with her Uncle Kevin. They always argued every single time he brought it up, and it didn't seem like he was going to back down anytime soon. The more Mabel talked about it, the more frustrated she got about her situation. Never before had her Uncle Kevin been so adamant about something.

"You have no say in this, Mabel," he said, crashing on the living room sofa. "It has been decided, it is final. Besides, what other option do you have?"

Mabel walked over to the living room sofa and stood in front of him. "I have plenty of other options."

Kevin scoffed. "Name one."

As she opened her mouth to speak, she instantly realized that she had nothing to say. Kevin had blocked any other options she had that could save her from an arranged marriage. He was working hand in hand with her enemy to make sure that she succumbed to their will. But she wasn't having any of it.

"Edgar Winthrop is not the man I want to spend the rest of my life with," Mabel whined, taking her seat by Kevin's side. "Come on, Uncle Kevin. Stop being blind to his faults. You know deep down that he is not a good man but you choose not to see it because it is convenient for you."

"Your father wasn't a good man until he met your mother," he argued. "Heck, no one liked him. But all of a sudden, your mother came along and he became a completely different person. I became the bad sibling. I don't care what you think of Edgar. You can deal with him when you get married. You know, change him as your mother did to my brother. You might even succeed in stealing Edgar away from his family so he never talks to his brother again, and then when you both end up dead, the castaway brother will be forced to take your child in and raise them."

Mabel dropped her shoulders and sighed. Kevin never liked her mother and he always made it clear. He blamed her for pulling her father away from him, and it was evident that Kevin still held a grudge against her father for not caring as much about him as he did before he got married. To make matters even worse, her parents passed away, and he felt saddled with the responsibility of taking care of her.

"I am not to blame for your relationship with my parents, Uncle Kevin," Mabel mumbled. "Besides, that isn't what we're discussing. We're talking about my future, and my life and I would prefer if I had a say in this. Why won't you listen to me when I tell you that I do not want to marry Edgar?"

"Because you don't have a choice. Edgar is a good man. Stop complaining. You should consider yourself lucky that he wants to take you off my hands."

Edgar Winthrop was a banker there in the town. He was a short, snobbish man that caused the hairs on her body to stand on end whenever he was close by. Edgar loved to talk about himself. Mabel was pretty sure that if he could, he'd marry himself too. He was self-centered and fastidious and he had a smirk that never failed to ruin her day whenever she saw it. Even if Mabel wanted to try and like the man, it was very difficult to do so. She couldn't even talk to him without making a face.

"I am an adult, and I'm very capable of making my decisions for myself."

"So, what would you rather do? What's your plan?" Kevin sneered, thinking that he had her now.

"I would much rather not get married."

"Now, that's a selfish thing to say. You're only thinking of yourself. Many other fine ladies in this town would be delighted to marry Edgar. You should be flattered that he wants to be associated with you, a woman who had absolutely nothing to offer him other than a pretty face."

Mabel inhaled deeply and turned to look away. All her life, she had dreamed of marriage. She imagined being with someone caring, compassionate... a real man. Someone that considered other people and did not only think of himself. Mabel was only twenty years old, and she was still trying to find her place in the world. She wasn't going to discover herself by Edgar's side. Edgar seemed like the kind of man that would trap her in a box and prevent her from doing anything other than what he wanted.

"Are we done talking about this?" Kevin asked.

"Uncle, please, will you just listen to me?" Mabel asked. "I know my prospects are limited at best, but this is not the way to go. At least, let me try to take control of my own life. Let me do this my way. Edgar isn't the kind of man that will ever be able to provide for me long-term. I'm certain of it."

"Mabel, you need to get married to someone so that I can make my journey to the West. I wish to forget all about this place and start my life afresh. Don't you understand this or are you just choosing to be stubborn?"

"At least let me live here then. Until I'm able to..."

"That is not an option. I will only leave West Virginia when you're married and not my problem anymore."

"Well, then let me come with you."

"Life isn't always about you!" he retorted, louder than necessary. "Part of the reason I'm going away is because of you, and I'm sick of this town. I'm going to start a new life, somewhere far from here and you're not going to ruin it. So, you will do as I say. I don't want to hear any more excuses, am I understood?"

"I'm not giving excuses; I'm trying to reason with you. I don't want to be trapped here in West Virginia as Edgar's bride. I will not marry such a self-centered man."

"You said it yourself. Your prospects are limited. I don't see you coming up with solutions, yet here you are, condemning a perfectly brilliant one. Edgar wants to marry you, and I see no problem with this, so you will marry him so I can live my life in peace, knowing that I'm not responsible for you any longer."

"There must be..."

He cut her off once more. "Don't you feel sorry for me? Even a little bit? I have taken care of you for years now, ever since you were twelve years old. I've been trapped with you, and you don't see me complaining about how unhelpful you have been to me. No. I learned to live with it because people have bad luck sometimes."

"Are you saying I was bad luck?" Mabel asked with a quivering voice. "I have done nothing to offend you, Uncle. I walk on eggshells just to make sure you have no reason to be offended by my actions. I bet you can't name one thing that I have done to wrong you."

"How about being born?" he retorted and rose to his feet. "You are marrying Edgar and that is final. I don't want to hear another word of this."

Mabel sat there with her head down and flinched when Kevin slammed the door shut. She couldn't understand why someone who was related to her by blood would hate her that much. Sometimes, she wondered if it was because she looked like her mother, Kevin's sworn enemy. They both had curly, dark blonde hair and the same blue eyes. Perhaps Kevin saw her mother in her, and that was the reason he chose to treat her so unkindly.

But it didn't change the fact that she was his niece. His brother's child. Not once had he treated her with compassion since the very first day she came into his life. Even though he wasn't as close to her father as he used to be before he got married, Kevin's behavior towards Mabel wasn't justifiable. Her father loved Kevin regardless and left everything to him. Kevin on the other hand always took every opportunity to talk badly about her mother.

It didn't help that Mabel had no other relatives in West Virginia. She knew no one else. Even though Kevin was cold towards her, she was consoled by the fact that she wasn't alone in the world. She at least had someone. But now that he was thinking of leaving and marrying her off to just anyone, Mabel feared that she was going to hate her life even more than she already did. What could she do?

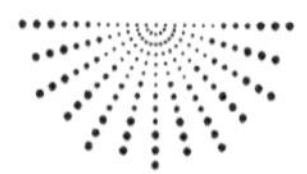

CHAPTER FOUR

"Hello, pretty lady, what can I help you with?"

"Do you have a prince charming, one that I can fall in love with in ten days and marry?"

Mabel and Greta, her best friend exchanged looks and started giggling. Greta Parker was the only friend she had in the town and the only person that understood her situation. They had known each other since she was twelve and they had been inseparable ever since. Greta's family owned a diner in the town, and Greta liked to help out whenever she could by waiting tables. Mabel liked to stop by and spend time with Greta whenever she could. It was a way to pass time and laugh for a bit, temporarily forgetting her plight.

"Is your uncle still insisting?"

Mabel groaned and threw her head back. "Yes. I don't know what to do at this point, Greta. I don't have a choice. When he leaves town, he's going to sell the house. I'll have nowhere to stay. To make things worse, he won't leave until I'm married to Edgar."

"You can't marry Edgar," Greta protested.

"I know!" Mabel groaned again. "I really don't want to, but I don't see another way out of this. You know I'm not against the idea of marriage, I've always dreamed of finding the love of my life and starting a family of my own. My memory might be foggy, but I remember just how much my parents loved each other. I want that for myself. Someone to always stick up for me, and love me. I want to be an important person in my partner's life. Not just... furniture like Edgar wants."

"I bet if you marry him, he'd get sick of you in a matter of months and start flirting with other women."

"I'd be lucky if he waits a few months. Edgar only wants a child from what I've heard. Not love. Oh, Greta, I'll be a prisoner if I marry him."

"I'm aware of that," she said. "You know I'd be more than happy to let you stay in my house, but there's nowhere for you to stay. My cousins are around and they're not leaving until after Christmas."

"You don't have to explain to me, Greta. I understand. Plus, your father is a friend of my uncle's, and I bet he won't take me in because of him. Believe me, I've thought about all my options."

Greta rapped her fingers on the table. "Would you have been fine with the idea of marriage if it was someone else?"

"If it was someone I had something in common with, then why not? If Edgar was half a decent man and if he actually cared for me, then I wouldn't be arguing with my uncle every single day. I do want to settle down, just not with him. I think it's high time I found a better life somewhere else."

Greta's eyebrows furrowed. "What do you mean?"

"I mean, maybe I should be considering prospects outside of West Virginia. I've lived here all my life and now that it seems like things are about to change for me, then what if I just... take the bull by the horn? It's my life, and I bet that if I come up with a plan for it, Uncle Kevin won't stop me. He's leaving anyway."

"We've been trying to think of a plan for weeks now. I'm sure your uncle is busy planning your wedding. What plan could you possibly come up with in a matter of weeks?"

"I don't know," Mabel mumbled. "But I believe something good is going to happen eventually. At least I'd like to believe so."

"Well, you know I'll always be here to support you with whatever decision you make. I just want you to be happy, Mabel, and I too believe that something good is coming your way. But in the meantime, we do need to think of a plan just in case your uncle decides to rush the wedding so he can leave."

Mabel giggled. "We should, actually. Do you have anything in mind? I just thought I'd pretend to be sick if that day ever comes."

"Uncle Kevin will see right through that. You know this. He might even bring the pastor to your bedside."

"That is true." She laughed and then proceeded to sigh. "Well, we'll think of something."

Greta nodded. "I have to tend to tables. Will you wait until I'm done with work for the day so we can take a stroll and talk more about the disaster going on in your life?"

"I'd like that," she answered with a smile. "Thank you, Greta."

Greta rose to her feet and as she walked away, she paused and turned back to the table. "Mabel?"

Mabel lifted her head. "Yes?"

"I agree. You should leave this town. The more I think of it, the more I'm sure that there's nothing left for you here. If your uncle leaves, nothing ties you here anymore."

"There's you," Mabel said.

"I'm not a good enough reason," Greta answered. "Plus, if I saw my opportunity, I'd leave too. As I said, I just want you to be happy. So, think of that when you're coming up with this plan for your life. Your happiness is all that matters. I'm sure that's what your parents would want for you. You're a beautiful lady, and you deserve more than a man like Edgar Winthrop."

Mabel smiled. "Thank you, Greta," she whispered. "I really needed to hear that."

Now seated alone, Mabel picked up the newspaper she had found on the table when she arrived and sat back to skim through it. She figured she needed to keep herself busy until Greta was ready for the stroll. She had been reading casually for a while until she got to the advertisement page. Mabel sat up and thoroughly read through each and every one. Sadly, she couldn't find anything that piqued her interest and was about to flip the page but she paused, something drew her to the last advert.

"Warm and industrious miner ready for a loyal, and loving wife," she mumbled. "I'm loyal... and I can be loving."

Before she stopped to think, Mabel found herself taking out the page in the newspaper. "Gray Rock, Colorado..."

The sound of an adventure to Colorado sounded very appealing to her. She was looking to take control of her own life. If she happened to meet this warm and industrious man that somehow ticked all her boxes with his attributes, and they eventually fell in love, it would be like a dream come true.

What if he is my prince charming?

CHAPTER FIVE

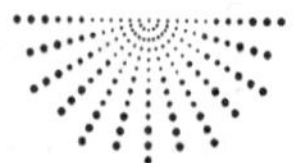

"*D*o you think it's too late to shop for new clothes for Grace, darling?" Eugene Tompkins asked.

Gloria giggled as she rocked Grace in her arms. "We already bought Grace's Christmas presents and clothes last month. We got her new shawls and you're building her a new bed. Christmas is two months away, dear. We still have some time."

"I know, but this is Grace's first Christmas with us. I should plan better. But I reckon it's never too late. I'll make sure to stop by the market tomorrow and get some of the things we need. We also need to get Steven some new clothes too. He's starting to outgrow the ones he has."

"First off, there is no need to apologize. We're both excited and I know we're going to have a lot of fun preparing for the season and celebrating it as a family. We'll do everything together. We'll make a list of the things we need first, before stopping by the mercantile to shop."

"All right. I'll do whatever you say."

Gloria smiled at him before turning her attention to the baby. There were times when she'd sit and compare her experience with Steven, and with his sister, Grace. Perhaps it was because she was rather young when she had Steven, but raising him had been awfully difficult. Her late husband did very little to help, and Gloria had been lost most of the time. It had not been easy, and back then, Steven happened to be the only source of joy in her life. He had been the reason she had kept herself together, and soon, she got the hang of motherhood.

However, it was different with Grace. Things were much easier. Gloria guessed it was because she had people around her this time. People that actually cared for her. A husband that loved her and friends that were always eager to help. Even Steven was happier than he had ever been. He was looking forward to Christmas, mainly because of all the presents people had promised him.

Speaking of Steven...

Gloria set Grace down on the sofa and stopped to think. Every time thoughts of Steven crossed her mind, she worried. Lately, Grace wasn't feeling well and she would cry at night, causing Gloria and Eugene to stay up, taking care of her. They were heaping so much attention on Grace that she worried Steven would be feeling left out. He had never complained, but Gloria feared that when he eventually did, it would break her heart.

"What is it?" Eugene asked, watching her. "You think it's too late to go Christmas shopping? I knew it. All the good stuff will have been taken."

Gloria chuckled and shook her head. "No, that's not it. I was thinking about Steven."

"What about Steven?" Eugene asked curiously.

Gloria sat up and cleared her throat. "Lately, I realized that we haven't been seeing to him that often, and I know it's because he goes to school during the day, but I can't help but feel like he's pulling away from us."

Eugene arched his eyebrows. "How do you mean?"

"Since I gave birth to Grace, she has become the center of our attention. Not that it's a bad thing. She's a baby, she needs our love and our attention. And I know how much you love Steven too, but-"

"But Steven had all that love and attention to himself before she came along and you're worried that he would think we've forgotten about him because we're concentrating a lot on Grace now."

"Exactly."

Eugene ran his hands through his hair and nodded. "I agree. I can't even recall the last time I took Steven to the mine. He used to love to go there. How do we fix this?"

"I'm not sure. I think we should probably sit him down and talk to him about it. We need to know how he truly feels first... before we proceed. What do you think?"

"That's a good idea. I think it's better to do it now before he shows any clear signs that he's hurt."

"I was thinking the same thing. I don't think I'll be able to bear it if he's the one that comes to me, sobbing that we're not paying attention to him like we used to."

Just then, Steven scurried into the room, back from school. He dropped his bag on the floor as he made his way to the sofa, giggling. He seemed excited about something. His hair was rough and he was sweating like he had been running.

"Steven, you're back," Eugene said before lifting him off the ground and placing him on his lap. "How was school today, my boy?"

"It was fine, thank you," he answered, still panting from all the running. "I made a friend today. His name is Edward. His sister is teaching him how to sew a ragdoll."

"A ragdoll?" Gloria asked. "Do you want to learn how to sew a ragdoll too?"

"No, I'm learning how to build a wooden truck."

"Oh, that's good too," Eugene said. "You seem excited about this. I like that."

"When I'm done making the wooden truck, and when Edward is done making the ragdoll, we're going to make a trade. Edward is going to give his little brother the truck, and I'll get Gracie the ragdoll. She's going to love it."

Gloria exchanged looks with Eugene and smiled. "I'm sure she's going to. You're a really thoughtful young boy, aren't you?"

"It's my Christmas present for Gracie," he continued. "Everyone's getting me a present, so I wanted to get her one too. So she can play with it."

Eugene patted Steven on the head. "You know we love you very... very much, don't you?"

Steven nodded, giggling.

"And you know you can ask me for anything in this world, and I'll climb the tallest mountain to get it for you, if I have to, right?" Eugene said.

"I don't need anything at the top of a mountain, Dad," he answered, still giggling. "I love you too."

"What about me? Don't I get an 'I love you' from my favorite boy?" Gloria asked, pouting.

Steven threw himself on her. "I love you, Mummy."

"I love you too."

Holding Steven in her arms, Gloria realized that she had been worried for nothing. She still made a mental note to pay more attention to Steven, but from what she could see, he was all right. Her kind, little boy was happy, what more could she ask for?

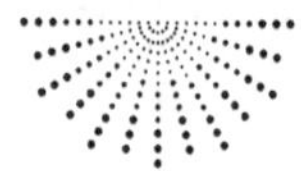

CHAPTER SIX

"Tree day!"

Drusilla turned to Jamison, her husband, who was now covering his face with a newspaper to hide his laugh. "I blame you for this," she said to him.

"What? It's adorable," he answered.

Tree day... was Carolyn's new favorite word. Jamison had repeated it to her so many times that she said it multiple times a day, constantly asking if it was tree day yet. Jamison had told Carolyn all about Christmas. About cutting down a tree, and decorating it with ornaments, then, of course, the food, the presents... and the snow. Now, it was all Carolyn looked forward to. She refused to talk about anything else and would only agree to eat her food if Drusilla assured her that 'tree day' was coming.

"I think it's adorable too, Drusilla," Carrie chimed in.

"I know it's adorable, but Carolyn keeps running around the house, asking about tree day. If Jamie didn't get her all excited about it, she wouldn't be yelling just that one phrase five times in one hour."

"The good news is that she's finally old enough to look forward to Christmas. Isn't that exciting? We can decorate the tree together, and bake together. Oh, we're going to have so much fun."

Drusilla rolled her eyes and smiled. "I don't doubt it. This is also going to be our first Christmas with Carl at the table. I can't wait."

"Me neither," Carrie answered.

"How is the sheriff?" Jamison asked, setting his newspaper down. "It's been a couple of days since I've seen him in person. Perhaps you both can stop by for dinner sometime this week."

"I'd like that. Carl has been quite busy at the office for the past couple of days. There have been several disputes and it's taking him longer than he imagined to solve them for people. Thinking about it, he spends so much more time at the sheriff's office than he does at home."

"He takes his work very seriously," Drusilla said. "That's admirable. Everyone in the town respects him too."

Carrie took Carolyn into her arms, nodding. "I'm glad he at least enjoys what he does."

Drusilla smiled at her mother-in-law. Carl Hill had been a great influence on her ever since they had gotten married. Carrie's smile had gotten brighter and she was happier than she had ever been. Before Carl came into Carrie's life, Drusilla worried that Carrie would feel lonely, living all by herself. This was why she made an effort to visit as much as she could, and spend time with Carrie so she could have some company. It was a relief that Carrie had someone by her side now. Someone that genuinely cared about her. It felt as if everything had fallen into place. Everyone was happy, Carolyn was walking and talking... Drusilla could smile and look forward to the Christmas season with a contented, and full heart.

"By the way, Carrie," Drusilla said, breaking the silence. "Jamie told me you're currently helping a miner find a bride. It's good to know that you're back to the business of matchmaking."

"Thank you," Carrie answered. "And yes, I am back and I don't intend on stopping anytime soon. His name is Zachary Warner. He likes to be called Zach."

"Zach's a bit rough around the edges, but he's a good man," Jamison chimed in. "He started working at the mine not long ago, but he takes the work there seriously even though he doesn't have regular work days like most of us."

"What was your first impression of Zach?" Carrie asked him. "When you first met him?"

Jamison paused to think. "Well, to be honest, when I first saw him, I thought he was a bit of an outlaw. I mean, you can't blame me, he has an intimidating look about him."

Drusilla chuckled. "He's built like Peter, except he's a bit bigger. I can understand why you'd think he's intimidating."

"He really is," he continued. "Plus, Zach barely spoke when he first started working at the mine. He used to work with horses, but he stopped to find other work. He really likes horses. When he finally started talking to us, he never stopped. He's very... expressive of his feelings and I like that about him."

"Unlike you," Carrie taunted him. "Remember how you were when Drusilla first came to Gray Rock?"

Drusilla giggled. "Oh, I remember. He couldn't even look me in the eye for days."

"All right, that's in the past. And that's not me anymore. Plus, we're talking about Zachary here. I think you did a good thing by helping him, Mother. He deserves your help. I think having someone by his side will help him a lot."

"Yes, I think so too," Carrie answered. "Thankfully, I've made some progress. I received a letter from a nice lady in West Virginia and I sent her a response yesterday. Hopefully, she's the one for Zach. He didn't want to spend Christmas alone this year, so if it turns out that this lady is truly the one for him, then I'll be so pleased."

"I hope she's the one too," Drusilla added. "But seeing as you have a solid track record, I don't think you have anything to worry about. Even if this lady turns out not to be the one for Zach, I know you'll still find him his match, no matter how long it takes. You're not one to give up. That's something I admire about you."

"Thank you, my dear," Carrie replied with a smile on her face. "You know me well. I'm up for any and every challenge. I'll be honest with you; at first, I didn't think I could do it. You see, Zach has his flaws too, but I'm hoping that once I secure him his bride, he'd be willing to change."

"You mean his looks?" Jamison asked. "Zach doesn't really pay a lot of attention to what he looks like. All he likes to do is work, and since he always gets his job done, no one seems to mind that he looks so unkempt."

Carrie shook her head. "Well, that has to change because he most certainly cannot meet a bride looking like that."

"What if he refuses to clean up?" Drusilla asked. "What if he sees nothing wrong with how he looks and refuses to change?"

"I doubt he'd refuse, dear," Jamison answered. "Zach takes instructions well. Since he came to Carrie for help, then I'm certain he'd listen to her advice if it means that he gets what he wants in the end. Plus, I remember how I was when you first came to Gray Rock. I instinctively started to pay attention to what I looked like any time I was around you. Zach will probably do the same."

Drusilla smiled. "I didn't know that."

"Of course, you didn't. I never admitted it to you. Plus, I didn't realize I was doing it until I noticed I was brushing my hair every single day and making sure I thoroughly washed and put on my best clothes whenever I got back from the mine. It's the little things you do when you want to impress someone."

Drusilla leaned into his arms and hugged him tightly. She had Carrie to thank for bringing Jamison her way and she was always going to be grateful for the family she had. Gone were the days when she feared that she'd be out of a job, and end up alone, with no one to love and no family to call her own. It had been the right decision to trust Carrie, and Drusilla was resting assured that Zachary was in good hands.

CHAPTER SEVEN

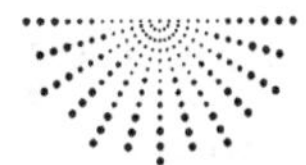

"**I** just don't understand. Why did Mrs. McCord choose to help you of all people?"

Zachary couldn't count how many times he had heard that statement in the past three days. He had been so excited to share the news that soon, he was going to get a bride. But his fellow miners didn't react how he had thought they would. Some of them laughed, some acted confused, while the others just chose not to believe him.

Regardless of their reaction, Zachary happily looked forward to the arrival of his bride. He had been right to go to Carrie for help. It didn't take her long to receive a response to the advert she had placed for him, and according to Carrie, his bride sounded sweet and eager to start a new life. It was all Zachary could think about. He went to bed every night with a smile on his face. Perhaps, there was hope for him after all.

"Perhaps she pitied him?" Tim, one of the miners said.

There were three of them seated with their backs against a tree. After a long morning working in the mine, a rest under the shade was much needed before they resumed working again.

Zachary kept his eyes closed and his lips shut. He didn't want to react to what the two miners, Tim and Larry were saying about him. He figured that they were just jealous of him because he dared to go after something he wanted, and they did not.

"Perhaps that's the reason," Larry said. "Because it makes no sense to me. I mean, there are plenty of other suitable people that Mrs. McCord could help."

"It's Mrs. Hill now," Tim corrected him. "Remember? She's married to the sheriff. Even she managed to make a good match for herself. The woman has some skill."

"Exactly. Why waste such skill on Zach here?" Larry asked and then turned to Zachary. "Are you really planning on meeting a bride looking like this, Zach? You might as well be wasting Mrs. Hill's efforts."

"I think it was a terrible idea telling you both about this," Zachary finally spoke. "You're just jealous that Carrie decided to help me and not you both."

Larry scoffed. "We never even asked for help. But even if we did, we'd have a better chance at finding and keeping a bride than you. Can't you see that we're just trying to advise you? You don't look like a man that is eager to find a bride. When was the last time you had a bath, or trimmed your beard? Or washed your hair? Changed your clothes? Wore different shoes? Do you really think your bride won't go running in another direction if she saw you looking like this?"

"Now, you're a decent man and all, Zach, but you don't look like it. Do you really plan on meeting your bride without a bath? If you intend to welcome her looking like this, then I don't think you're actually ready to be committed to someone."

Zachary fully opened his eyes and turned to them. "I don't understand. What do my looks have to do with anything?"

Larry let out a frustrated sigh and groaned. "I now truly believe that Mrs. Hill is wasting her time on you."

"There is no reason to talk about me like this. Is it a crime that I shared something I'm really excited about with the both of you? All you've done since you found out that Carrie's helping me, is taunt me at every chance you get. I don't appreciate it and I would like it if you both forget whatever I said to you and move on from it."

"Fine, suit yourself," Larry said. He and Tim rose to their feet and walked away, mumbling to themselves.

Zachary had not thought about it. He never paid attention to what he looked like because it never mattered to him. But now that Carrie had reassured him that he was going to get a bride soon, maybe it was time for a change? Maybe Larry and Tim were right. What if his bride saw him and ran the other way?

"Don't let them get to you."

Zachary lifted his head and saw Peter Quinn, one of the other miners approaching him. Peter sat by his side, exhausted from all the work he had done.

"Hello, Peter," Zachary greeted him. "How are you? And how is your family?"

"We're fine, thank you for asking. My wife is still pregnant but she's going to be put to bed any day now, so that's exciting... but at the same time, nerve-wracking.

The doctor advised that she stays in bed as much as she can, but she always has to pee, and it makes it hard to follow the doctor's orders. I'm just glad she was able to carry the baby for this long."

Zachary nodded with a bright smile spread across his face. This was the kind of conversation he liked to listen to. Hearing Peter speaking about his pregnant wife reminded Zachary of his sister, Peggy when she had been pregnant. It was a time he wasn't ever going to forget.

"Do you want it to be a boy or a girl?" Zachary asked. "My sister, Peggy wanted a girl when she was pregnant. I recall holding her baby in my arms. It had been a boy, and I had no idea how I was going to tell her when she had already made ragdolls and pink clothes."

"How did she react when she found out it was a boy?"

"She was so happy, that she cried. Turned out, it didn't matter to her at all. She wanted a girl, but she was happy with a boy too."

Peter chuckled. "Well, I just want a healthy baby. Regardless of what we get. I'd be equally happy with a boy, as I would be with a girl."

"That's the spirit. It doesn't matter. A baby will always be a blessing. No matter the sex."

"I agree," Peter said and sighed. "Zach, I know what Carrie is doing for you. She did the same for me and that's the reason I'm happy today."

Zachary nodded. "I heard you were one of the first persons she helped find a bride."

"I was," he answered.

"Let me ask you something, Peter. If you don't mind," Zachary continued. "Did you change anything about yourself before you received your bride?"

Peter paused to think. "At that moment, no. I didn't. But if you're asking me this because of what Larry and Tim were telling you, then it's different. I won't lie to you, Zach. You're a good man, but perhaps you should consider cleaning up a bit. It would show your willingness to accept change and it would be a great boost to your confidence."

Zachary lowered his head and stared at his dirty hands. He clicked his tongue and sighed. Although Larry and Tim didn't say it nicely, they were right. The fact that he didn't care so much about what he looked like didn't mean that his bride wouldn't care too. If all went according to plan, she was going to travel all the way from the East. It wouldn't speak well of him if he didn't put in any effort to look good, and it would insult Carrie's efforts.

"You think I should cut my hair?" Zachary asked Peter.

Peter nodded. "I do. I'm sure that under all that hair and raggedy clothes, is a fine, hardworking young man. You'll garner more respect if you changed how you looked, changed your clothes, and your boots too, they are a bit holey. Starting a family is a big responsibility and it demands a lot."

"You're right. I should get rid of this beard too. I don't know... I figured I'd just throw on some neat clothes when my bride arrived, but I realize now, that it's more than that. I need to impress her by putting some effort into the way I look."

"That's a good place to start," he told him. "I'll help you."

"Thank you, Peter. Truly, I'm grateful."

Zachary rubbed his palms together nervously. He wasn't sure how he'd look without his beard and with shorter hair, but if everyone was claiming that it needed to be done, then he would be stupid not to listen. It was time he paid attention to the things that mattered.

The last thing he wanted was to scare his bride away. What would he do if that happened?

CHAPTER EIGHT

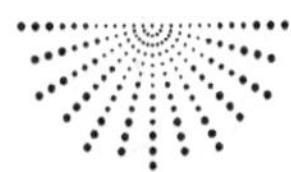

"So, you really are leaving?"

Saying goodbye to Greta was more difficult than Mabel had imagined. She was happy that she was leaving, but at the same time, she was going to miss Greta a great deal. Greta was the only friend she had managed to make in the town, and the thought of not seeing her again caused Mabel's eyes to sting. But it was for the greater good. Mabel was leaving to start a new life, somewhere far from West Virginia, with someone she chose to be with. Her life was going to be different; she was going to have control over her actions, and nothing was going to stop her from finding happiness.

"It's for the best, Greta," she answered. "I think I'll be happy there in Gray Rock. At least I wouldn't have to marry Edgar anymore."

"And this man... you're certain of his intentions?"

Mabel sighed. "I can't be completely certain, but... the woman that I first sent a letter to sounded confident that I will find a match in this town. Apparently, she's a matchmaker in Colorado. She'd know what to do, don't you think?"

"Don't trust too easily," Greta told her. "If anything feels off, or if it seems like they're trying to deceive you, then come back home. Don't wait. We'll think of something. At least then, perhaps your uncle won't be here in town anymore to control you."

"I have a feeling I won't be coming back here," Mabel said. "It will work out with this man. It has to. I have a good feeling about it. Even if things don't work out, I'll figure out a plan for my life there. But it's like you said. There's nothing here for me anymore."

Greta nodded. "That's true. You'll write to me when you can?"

"Most definitely. I'll write to you as soon as I arrive and tell you all about the town. I pray that you find happiness too, Greta. You deserve it."

"Who knows? If things work out so well for you, I might just write to this matchmaking woman and ask her to find me a real man as you did. I might even come looking for you in Colorado if I get tired of this place."

Mabel giggled. "You can do whatever you want. As long as you're happy."

Greta giggled too. "What did your uncle say when you told him? I bet he was glad you were leaving, wasn't he?"

Mabel shook her head. "He was upset. Very upset. He yelled at me, saying I was only doing this to spite him. He said people were going to call him a liar because he made a promise to Edgar and he couldn't keep that promise. He said a lot, Greta, but in the end, he said he didn't care. As long as I was gone and he didn't have to take care of me anymore."

Greta scoffed. "As if he ever really took care of you. You've been taking care of yourself since you were a child, Mabel. You do everything in that house. That's why I'm certain that you'll be fine by yourself. I'm sure of it. You make good choices, and you'll do what's best for you. This is your life to live."

"Thank you, Greta," she replied with a quivering voice. "I'll miss you."

Greta hugged Mabel tightly. "I'll miss you too. Take care of yourself."

"I will. Take care of yourself too."

"I will."

After hugging for a full minute, Mabel got into the stage-coach and headed for the station. She waved Greta goodbye until the stagecoach took a turn and she couldn't see her anymore. There were tears in her eyes, but also a smile on her face. Something had changed for her. Even though she had barely left the town, she felt at ease. There was hope for happiness.

Mabel thought about her uncle. She recalled the look on Kevin's face when she told him she was leaving West Virginia. It was far-fetched to wish that he would at least miss her. But he didn't look like he would. After he got over the fact that he was angry, he looked relieved. Glad that he was free of her.

Even though Kevin didn't react the way Mabel would have preferred him to, she was going to miss him a great deal. She made a mental note to write to him when she could and send him aid if he needed it. Since he too was planning on moving away, she figured it was best to write soon, so he could send her his new address.

Mabel shook her head, in a bid to clear her mind. She was very excited about the prospects before her and it was all she wanted to think about. Nothing else. There was someone out there who wanted to spend the rest of his life with her. It was all Mabel needed. She felt optimistic. Now that she was in complete control of her own life, things were going to be different. She wasn't going to walk on eggshells or pretend that she was all right when she was not.

"It'll be different," she whispered to herself.

Zachary Warner. A local miner in Gray Rock, Colorado. Mabel had exchanged a few letters with him and it turned out that they had a lot in common. He was really keen on finding a wife and starting a family, and she too wanted the same for herself. A family. From the letters, Mabel could tell that he was a nice man. He wasn't asking for much.

Soon, the stagecoach came to a halt and she stood in front of the train. Mabel took in a deep breath. This was her only plan for her life and she was hopeful. She figured nothing could be worse than her life in West Virginia. However, she had never traveled before, and although the thought of it was terrifying, she was calm, knowing that there was light at the end of this particular tunnel.

CHAPTER NINE

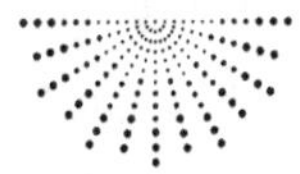

Zachary was nervous. He had no reason to be, but he couldn't help it. He wasn't used to letting people help him. Although he had known Peter for a while, it still felt strange that the man would offer his help so freely.

Peter had come to him that morning and he had offered to take him to someone that could give him a haircut. According to him, it was a friend of his that partially owned the mercantile in town. Once Zachary had heard the words 'haircut' and 'offer' he instantly hopped on the opportunity. Before Peter's offer, he had not worked out what he would do with his hair. It was a mess, he normally just hacked a bit off it, if it was annoying him. He had to look better, he had to clean himself up, but he had no idea how to do it, and Mabel, his bride was already on her way to Gray Rock.

After talking to Peter two days ago about his appearance, Zachary had tried to tidy himself up. It wasn't a lot, but he washed all his good clothes, threw out his holed boots, and bought some new ones, and he took a long bath to clean all the dirt from his body. Even though he had spent an entire day cleaning up, it still felt like he was ignoring the elephant in the room. His hair. He had figured he'd get a pair of scissors and cut it himself but thankfully, Peter came to his rescue.

"Can I ask you a personal question, Zach?" Peter said, breaking the silence.

"Sure. Ask away."

"Why do you want to get married? I know the obvious reason. To start a family of your own, to get rid of the loneliness. But what are your reasons?"

Zachary bit his lower lip. It wasn't something he had thought about, he just wanted a wife. "Why did you get married?"

"I asked you first."

Zach shrugged. "I know, but I want to hear from you first. You already said the obvious reason... the ones I would have said, so tell me your other reasons. Why did you decide that it was time to get married?"

Peter inhaled deeply. "Let's see... I was at my friend's wedding. Jamison McCord. It was the day I realized I was ready, hence, why I can never forget it. Before that day, my friend, Jamie didn't smile a lot. He rarely expressed his emotions and we used to tease him that he would never find a bride to marry because he couldn't even talk to women. But he met his wife, Drusilla, and he became a totally different person. On his wedding day, the smile on his face was one I had never seen since I'd known him. He was genuinely happy and in love. I'd never fallen in love before but seeing what it did to my friend, I wanted it too. So, I guess I'd say that was the day I decided. I wanted to experience love. To love and to be loved. That's the reason I approached Carrie in the first place."

"Whoa," was all Zach could say.

"Your turn."

Zachary nodded. "Well, I guess the realization hit me when I was lying alone in bed, reading my sister's most recent letter. I started to wonder what I was doing with my life. You don't realize it, but time is slipping away. I was lost in this world I had created for myself in my head. You see, I don't have a lot, Peter. My house isn't the best place to start a family. I need to fix it. I don't earn a lot of money, so I need another source of income, and I don't know what it feels like to love someone that's not family, but hopefully, I'll learn that soon enough. My point is, I was scared that I wasn't ready for a family, but I still found myself searching for Carrie. It didn't matter. I guess I'm desperate, and I'm willing to do whatever I can to make it work. I'd do anything. I'll admit that I didn't think it would happen so quickly, but I won't run from this or shy away from what I've always wanted. My point is, I want to get married because I need someone by my side. I want a wife to support me... but I will support her too. To love me as I love her. I'd like a chance to be thrilled about something too. To feel..."

"Alive?" Peter asked.

"Something like that."

Peter nodded. "It's good you know what you want. Hopefully, this bride is exactly what completes you."

"Thank you so much, Peter. And thank you for offering to help. You didn't have to, but you did and I'm truly grateful that you want to help."

"It's my pleasure, really."

They arrived at the mercantile and seated at the front desk was a young lady, putting up Christmas decorations on the wall. They were bits of painted wood and made the place look so jolly. She was so distracted by it that she didn't hear them come in. It was only when Peter softly knocked on the counter that she spun around to look at them.

"Good morning, Tillie," Peter greeted her. "You seem very excited this morning."

Tillie smiled sheepishly. "Yes, I am excited. We decided to spend the day decorating the store. Saul and Lucille just went inside to get some more of these ornaments we made. We're going to put a big tree right over here too. I'm so looking forward to Christmas."

"I can see that," Peter replied. "Is Wyatt here?"

"Peter," a man that Zachary presumed to be Wyatt said as he appeared from the back. "Good morning. What a pleasant surprise. Did you come here to see me? Or..."

"How're you, Wyatt?" Peter questioned.

Wyatt stood by Tillie's side and took her hand. "I'm very well, thank you. Is everything all right?"

"Everything's fine. I did come here to see you. Actually, I came to ask for a favor, if you don't mind."

"Absolutely. Tell me what you need."

Peter glanced at Zachary. "Would you mind cutting his hair? I saw you give Eugene a haircut the other day and it was good. I was wondering if you'd be willing to do the same for Zachary over here. He's meeting his intended bride today."

A smile formed on Wyatt's face. "Carrie?"

"Yes, she arranged it," Peter answered.

"I'd be more than happy to cut your hair, Mr. Zachary," Wyatt said to him.

"Oh, please. It's just Zach," he answered, stuttering. "Thank you. I'd really appreciate it."

"Come. Sit, please," Tillie said, gesturing at a chair by the counter.

Zachary could tell that they were assessing him. He didn't mind, and from the smile on their faces, he guessed that he was in safe hands. They seemed happy to hear that he was getting a bride and it baffled him because they had just met.

Unlike most of the miners who scoffed when he told them, these people seemed thrilled by the news. Perhaps, it was because they knew Carrie well enough to trust her skills. Whatever it was, Zachary was glad he was getting some help.

"So, where is your new bride from?" Tillie asked.

"Uh, West Virginia, ma'am," Zachary answered. "Her name is Mabel Mason."

"What a pretty name. Congratulations. I know it's a bit too early to be saying this, but I think you need to hear it. If Carrie thinks she has gotten a match for you, then just trust that it will work out well. Take her other matches for instance."

Zachary chuckled awkwardly. "Well, thank you. It is a big thing for me. So, I guess congratulations are in order."

"My point exactly," she continued. "Where will she be staying before the wedding?"

"Carrie's house. I was so relieved when Carrie told me Mabel could stay with her and the sheriff. I'll make sure to see her every day. I intend to take her to nice places, but return her to the sheriff's house at the end of the day."

As they talked, Wyatt and Peter walked back into the room with the tools they needed to cut Zachary's hair. They took him to the front of the shop and sat him down. Soon, Wyatt began to cut off his hair.

Zachary drew in a nervous, deep breath as he heard the scissors cutting. He had mixed feelings coursing through his body, but one thing he was sure of, was that this was the right thing to do.

"When do you plan on getting married?" Wyatt asked.

"As soon as we're ready," he replied. "I need to work on my home, make it nicer for Mabel to stay in. I need to figure out how to bring more money into the house... there are still some things that need to be put in place, but I'm working on them."

"That's good. At least you're better off than me when I went to Carrie seeking a bride," Wyatt said. "I was living in a shack. I had no job either, and I kind of looked like you a bit."

His statement caused them all to laugh. "Seeing as things turned out well for you despite that, I find it reassuring."

"You should be reassured," Wyatt continued. "Just trust Carrie. There must be some similarity between you and your bride for her to decide that you are a good match."

"I've been meaning to ask," Peter chimed in. "What will you be wearing to meet Mabel?"

"I picked out a nice white shirt, and a pair of nice pants too. They're at home."

Peter snorted. "A nice white shirt? You own a nice white shirt, Zach?"

Zachary tilted his head slightly. "Well... yes. I do. It's not new, but it'll do."

"No, it won't. I have a nice suit at home that'll fit you. Of course, I don't wear it. It's too big for me and... well, where will I wear it to? It was a gift that has been sitting in my house collecting dust. I figured you can use it today."

"Oh, Peter. What is he? A banker?" Wyatt asked. "Isn't a suit a bit too much? I mean, if he's meeting the woman he's going to spend the rest of his life with, shouldn't he look casual... like he always does."

"No, I think I like the idea of a suit," Zachary chimed in. "I'll look professional and serious. I need Mabel to know that I'm serious about her and not playing any games. A suit will do just that for me. Thank you, Peter, I can't thank you enough."

"See? He gets it," Peter said. "We'll stop by my house after the haircut and dress up."

"All right," Zachary said, feeling much better about the plan.

"What about your wagon? Is it in good shape?" Peter asked.

"It is. I acquired it not long ago and I barely use it," he answered.

"Remember to be yourself, Zach," Tillie said to him. "She will want to see the man she corresponded with. Don't try anything different, be yourself. Be the same person you introduced to her through your letters."

Zachary nodded. "I will. Thank you."

"And don't be awkward," Wyatt added. "Ladies don't like that. You can be shy, but don't be dismissive. Ask questions and listen to her replies so you can ask follow-up questions. And remember to always be polite."

"I will," Zachary said, feeling a lump form in his throat. There was so much to remember.

Meeting Wyatt and Tillie increased Zachary's anxiety. He had managed to convince himself that it wasn't a big deal. It was just going to be a casual meeting where he introduced himself and then took her to Carrie's house.

But now that he had spoken to Wyatt and Tillie about it, coupled with the fact that they were cutting his hair and talking about his outfit, Zachary was getting nervous. He had to make a good impression. He needed to do this; his future depended on it. What would he do if it all fell through?

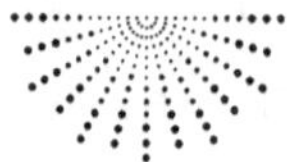

"Finally."

Mabel felt dizzy and her stomach rumbled. The trip to Gray Rock was a very long, and bumpy one, and now that it was all over and she was standing on the side of the road, she felt a bit nauseous. She was excited, a bit nervous, but also on the verge of throwing up. That would not make a good first impression. She almost chuckled at the thought.

"Calm yourself," she whispered, shutting her eyes and taking in a deep breath. "You're about to meet him."

It felt surreal, standing in another town, far from her home. Everything was strangely different about the place. The air felt different, even the rays of the sun felt a bit harsher too. It looked like it had snowed earlier that day, judging from the snow-covered path. Mabel loved when it snowed. It was one of her favorite things to watch.

"Excuse me? Miss Mabel Mason?"

A gasp slipped from her lips as she turned upon hearing her name. "Yes?"

Mabel lifted her head and her eyes fell on a tall man with a big build wearing a very smart suit. He was clean-shaven, with short brown hair and brown eyes. He bowed as soon as she met his gaze and extended his hand to her.

"My name is Zachary Warner. Are you Miss Mason?"

"Just Mabel is fine."

Mabel couldn't take her eyes off him. She felt reluctant to take his hand, but she did it anyway. He reminded her of Edgar. She had no idea why it was Edgar that popped into her head at that very moment, but Zachary seemed very similar to the man. He was so rigid, with similar clothes, and a straight face that looked a little intimidating.

"Well, it's nice to meet you, Mabel," Zachary said. "Welcome to Gray Rock."

"Thank you," she answered, shaking off the thoughts that crowded her mind. Even though he bore some resemblance to Edgar, it wasn't him. She had come to like Zachary through the letters they exchanged and she figured it was probably awkward since this was the first time they were meeting face-to-face.

"Thank you, Zach," she answered. "May I call you Zach? It's short for Zachary, so I figured…"

"It's fine. Everyone calls me Zach," he said and placed both hands behind him.

An awkward silence ensued between them. Mabel took in a breath and tried to stretch, she had been couped up in the stagecoach for many hours, while Zachary stared into space. It seemed like he was waiting for her to say something, or thinking of his next words. Mabel wanted to say something, but she was finding it hard to get past the fact that he was dressed like Edgar.

On the upside, he was as handsome as she had imagined he'd be. He was a bit taller than she had thought and he towered over her. She liked his eyes, but he didn't give her enough time to stare into them. Mabel wasn't sure if he couldn't look her in the eye, or if he wouldn't.

"So, how was your journey to Gray Rock? How'd you like the town?" Zachary asked.

"Uh... I haven't seen the town but the journey was long, and... bumpy," she stuttered. "It wasn't as smooth as I thought it would be, to be honest. Have you traveled far before?"

Zachary responded by shaking his head.

"Oh, lucky you," She smiled but he didn't return it. "Well, it gets a bit tiring, you know, sitting in the train for so long. Then when I got to the end of the line, I took a long stagecoach ride here and I felt nauseous at one point but I'm fine now. I think."

"I'm sorry," he said, massaging his nape. "It was a stupid question."

"No, there's no need to be sorry. It was a good question. I would just really like to go somewhere private and maybe talk for a bit? We could get to know each other a bit better. I must admit, you're not exactly how I imagined you'd look," she confessed.

Zachary lifted his eyebrows. "I'm sorry."

"No, there's no need – I wasn't trying to...."

Mabel bit her lower lip and lowered her head. This was not going according to plan. It seemed like she was the one trying to make conversation and Zachary wasn't interested.

"What do you want to do?" Mabel asked him. "Do you have somewhere we could go and talk privately? I think our conversation is taking this weird turn because we're in public."

"That's my wagon over there," he said, pointing at the vehicle. "We'll head to Carrie's house now to meet her family for a meal. She'd like to welcome you herself."

"Oh, all right. That's nice of her. Are you both really close?"

Zachary took her bags and led her to the wagon hastily. "I won't say we're close," he answered. "Carrie helps people meet their brides and I went to her. If it wasn't for Carrie, I wouldn't have the honor of meeting you."

Mabel stifled a smile. "That's a nice thing to say."

Finally, a smile formed on his face, causing Mabel to sigh in relief. It was a short one, but she was glad she saw it. He cleared his throat and helped her into the wagon.

As they rode through the town, Mabel got a better look at the place. It bore some similarity to her town in West Virginia, but it was much smaller. Gray Rock was bustling, men were walking in groups, others riding or driving by. There were a few women but mostly men and it had recently snowed.

"I like the snow," Mabel said, attempting to make small talk. "Do you like the snow too?"

"Yes." Zachary nodded. "It's one of the reasons Christmas is my favorite holiday. I have this small window in my room and a pretty heavy blanket. On the days when it snows and I don't have to work, I would snuggle underneath the covers and just watch the snow fall through my window. I find it to be relaxing."

Mabel nodded. "I like watching it snow because it's relaxing too. Hopefully, we'll be married before Christmas so we can spend the holiday together, watching it snow. I think I'd like that."

Zachary glanced at her and shifted where he sat. "We can only wed once we set up a proper house."

"A proper house?"

Zachary tightened his grip on the reins and concentrated on the path in front of him. Mabel couldn't tell what he meant by that. Didn't he have a place to live? Wasn't he expecting to get married soon? Was that the reason he wasn't putting enough effort into talking to her?

What have you gotten into, Mabel?

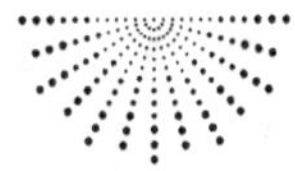

"Thank you so much for having me, ma'am."

"Please. Call me Carrie, and welcome to Gray Rock. I hope the journey wasn't so stressful. You must be tired."

It felt very strange, having all those faces smiling down at her. There was Carrie, the matchmaker. It was shocking to discover that she was a grandmother. She looked barely middle-aged and very agile. There was Drusilla, the daughter-in-law. She was beautiful, and she seemed nice. Then, there was Jamison, Carrie's only son and Drusilla's husband. He looked like Carrie. Mabel could see the resemblance. They had a daughter called Carolyn, but she was asleep in Carrie's room. Apparently, the sheriff was supposed to join them for dinner, but he was at his office and would join them later.

"Oh, I think I'm hungrier than I am tired," Mabel answered. "Thank you again for the warm reception."

"You're welcome," Drusilla answered. "Please make yourself comfortable. If you need anything, let me know."

"Thank you."

Dinner was ham steak with potato dumplings in a cream sauce. Mabel tried not to get too excited, but she couldn't recall the last time someone prepared a homemade meal for her. It made her comfortable knowing that these people were genuinely happy to see her. They ate and talked about Gray Rock. Drusilla filled her in on the kind of people in the town, and how she came to Gray Rock in the first place.

"So, tell us about yourself, Mabel," Drusilla said in the middle of dinner. "What's your story? What brought you to Gray Rock?"

Mabel set her fork down and interlocked her fingers. "Well, there's not much to tell. In fact, I'm surprised that I'm here right now, but I believe that good things happen, you just need faith. I'm my parent's only child.

They passed away when I was twelve. Since then, I've been living with my uncle."

"I'm so sorry to hear that," Carrie said. "It must have been difficult losing both of them at such a young age."

"Oh, it was," she answered, forcing a smile. "Living with my uncle was difficult too. He controlled everything that I did. He has this resentment towards my parents that apparently, their deaths did not assuage. When I first moved in with him, he was angry all of the time. I used to think that the reason for his anger was the fact that he missed my father and he didn't know how to express it. But then, he got even angrier over the years, and it just didn't make sense anymore that he refused to let it go. I think he was more upset because of me. Having to take care of me when he never planned on having children of his own. I tried my best to please him and now that I think about it, it worked to an extent because since I gave him no reason to be upset, he didn't have anything specific to yell at me for. The only thing he could yell about was my parents, and how I should have never been born in the first place."

"Goodness, he sounds awful," Drusilla said.

"He was." Mabel nodded. "But to an extent, I kind of understand him. It must have been difficult for him to accept that his brother was no more. I was a constant reminder of it."

"Don't put this on yourself," Zachary said.

Mabel felt a hand on herself and she turned to the side to see Zachary staring at her so intently. He had a sorry look on his face as he squeezed her hand into his. Seeing him show such compassion softened something inside her. This was the Zachary she had hoped to meet when she arrived in town. It was the Zachary she had imagined when she read his letters.

"It's not your fault and you don't need to try and understand him," Zachary whispered to her. "I too lost my parents at a young age. If I recall correctly, I was thirteen years old when they passed away. Life was hard. Pretty difficult. My sister and I tried our best to survive, but there were days when we'd go without eating. There were days when I was lost and I had no idea what to do to make ends meet. I trapped, hunted, and did odd jobs. A few people took pity on us but they didn't have a lot. I started working at the silver mines at sixteen. I did what I could to earn some money and keep food on the table. It was tough, but I never blamed my parents for anything. It's not their fault that they died. It's life. We deal with it. Take every day as it comes. I remember being bullied for a while, but I never let it get to me. With time, it passed and I'm just a normal miner now."

Mabel placed her other hand over his and smiled. "And I thought I had it rough."

"You did. Your experience is yours, and mine is mine. Both are equally heartbreaking. Don't blame yourself for what you can't control."

"Where's your sister now? Do you both still live together?"

Zachary shook his head. "She's married now. To a nice man. They moved to California and are happy together. They have a daughter too. She turned a year old a few months ago."

"That's so nice. Do they come visiting?"

"No." He shook his head. "It hasn't been that long since they left. Plus, if anyone is to visit, I should go visit them. We exchange letters though. I get a letter from Peggy very frequently. She likes to keep me informed and remind me that I'm not getting any younger, hence, I should be considering settling down. Peggy is actually one of the reasons why I want to start a family. I see how happy it makes her, and I'd like to be happy too."

"Me too," Mabel whispered. "That's why I came all the way to the West. In search of happiness. And to get away from being under my uncle's thumb. But mostly for happiness and a family." She dropped her head as heat hit her cheeks.

Zachary chuckled. "Well, I'm glad we want the same thing. Hopefully, we'll find it in each other."

This made her feel so much better. This was the Zachary she had longed to meet. He was indeed kind, and compassionate. Mabel liked how he wasn't shy to express what he was feeling. He knew hardship and he spoke from the heart. What more could she ask for?

CHAPTER TWELVE

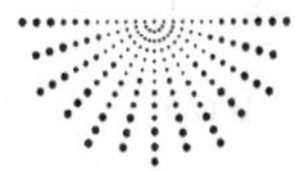

*S*hould I take his arm?

After dinner, Carrie suggested that Zachary take Mabel for a stroll before dessert was served. Zachary seemed to be reluctant at first, but he eventually succumbed to her will. They walked down the path and the distance between the both of them bothered Mabel. They were supposed to be getting to know each other, and yet Zachary was acting like a stranger again.

Mabel had thought that his brief show of emotion at the dinner table was the real him. She had hoped it would be. However, seeing as Zachary had gone back to his shy self, she couldn't help but wonder if this was the real him, or if he was holding his true self back for some reason.

"Have you lived in this town all your life?" Mabel asked him.

"Not really. My parents moved here from California when I was little. That's where I'm originally from, but all the memories I have, are from this place. So, you could say I've lived here all my life… as I don't remember anywhere else."

"Oh, that's nice. Before this, I'd never left West Virginia. I was born there, and up until I saw your advert in the paper, I thought I was going to spend the rest of my life there."

"When did you realize that you wanted to pursue your happiness somewhere else?" Zachary asked. "A friend of mine asked me why I wanted to get married. Apart from the obvious reason for wanting to start a family. He also asked me when I realized that I knew I was ready. Can I ask you the same question? When did you realize?"

Mabel sighed. "When I accepted the fact that I had no other option. I've always wanted to start a family. It has been a dream of mine since I was little. I used to watch children stroll past my house with their parents. I'd see them Christmas shopping, and decorating their trees outside the house. You know, I used to hate Christmas?"

Zachary turned to her. "What? Why? I love Christmas."

"I hated Christmas. I used to dread the day because I always ended up crying. Everyone was always so happy during the holidays. Families come together, from different parts of the country. People pray at dinner tables, laugh, talk, eat... give gifts. I, on the other hand, used to lay in bed and imagine all these things happening to me because they never did. My uncle wouldn't even cut down a tree for us to decorate and if I went out of my way to try and bring the Christmas spirit into our home, I'd be giving him something to yell about. Christmas was always a regular day at my house. The only time I actually enjoyed the holiday was when I spent it at Greta, my best friend's house. My point is, I didn't want to be so alone anymore. I wanted to start my own traditions, fall in love, raise children, and take control and responsibility for my own life. If I remained in West Virginia, I would never break away from my uncle's hold. Never. He had already planned out my life in such a way that he didn't have to be responsible for me anymore. It's my life, I should have a say in how I want to live it."

"I agree," he answered. "I understand that feeling of loneliness during the holidays. In fact, my realization came one night while I was lying in bed. It was too quiet. It felt like I was lying in a casket."

Mabel giggled. "A casket?"

"I kid you not. I felt suffocated and I said, enough! I don't want to live like this and I'm not spending another Christmas alone. I needed to take a step and change the course of my life. So, here we are."

"I'm glad you took that step," Mabel said. "You saved me too."

Feeling bold all of a sudden, Mabel tiptoed and placed a peck on Zachary's cheek. Her action caused him to abruptly stop in his tracks and his cheeks flushed crimson. He felt it too and quickly turned away from her to hide them.

"I can't wait for us to get married," Mabel said. "Then we can have more time alone and talk all about our lives, and our past. I have a lot of stories that I'd really like to share with you."

Zachary cleared his throat and continued to walk. "I have to tell you something, Mabel."

Mabel tensed on hearing the serious tone of his voice. "What is it?"

"I have to admit that the other miners that I work with are far more well-to-do than I am currently. I don't have a lot of working days at the mine; hence, I don't earn that much. So, right now, I'm afraid I don't have much to give. But…"

"That doesn't matter to me, Zach," Mabel said, taking his hand. "I didn't come here to find a man that's well off or one that doesn't lack anything. I came all this way to build a life with a man that I can love. That comes with obstacles, self-discovery, and trust. You don't need to try to impress me, Zach. Don't pretend to be something you're not. I'll accept you for who you are, and we can grow together. You just need to show me the real you so I know what I'm working with. That's what a marriage is, isn't it? I mean, it takes a lot of effort to start a family."

Zachary gave her a firm nod before he stiffened and took a step back. "We should probably go back inside. It would be rude to keep them waiting."

"But we've only been walking for a short while. Carrie said to take a nice, long stroll," Mabel protested.

"I'm sure she didn't mean that. We should go back and have dessert."

Mabel exhaled quietly and reluctantly nodded. "If you wish."

It didn't seem wise to argue with him over something so trivial, even though Mabel wanted to spend more time with him, talking. She had no idea what she had said to make Zachary retreat back into his shell and it saddened her that he was quiet again. It made it difficult to figure him out. It seemed as though he was holding his true self back, and Mabel couldn't understand why.

CHAPTER THIRTEEN

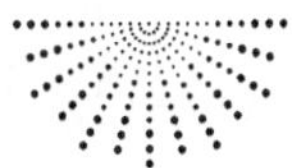

1 WEEK LATER...

Zachary looked down at his shirt for the umpteenth time and readjusted his hat. He had finally put on his white shirt after he brought it out weeks ago to wear. Jamison had gifted him the cowboy hat the day before and Zachary couldn't wait to show it to Mabel. He had planned a stroll with her for the day and even picked up some wild roses on the way because he figured it would impress her.

Mabel had affected him the way he had thought her presence in his life would. She was like a breath of fresh air. A beautiful and kind breath of fresh air. Sometimes,

Zachary questioned himself. He wasn't sure someone as lowly as he deserved a lady so beautiful and kind-hearted as Mabel. She didn't ask for anything and she clearly loved his company.

It made Zachary wonder if she would have reacted the same way if he hadn't shaved his beard and trimmed his hair. Peter, Wyatt, and Tillie had asked him to be himself when he met Mabel, but for some reason, he didn't heed their words. He had created another personality for himself when he saw Mabel standing on the side of the road. Zachary had no idea what he was pretending to be, but to his mind, he was a calm and collected individual who didn't speak much and always listened. Wyatt had said ladies liked men that listened.

However, with every day that he spent with Mabel, he found himself falling back into old habits. Larry, one of the miners used to tease him about how much he talked. Zachary figured Mabel wouldn't like a vulnerable man, so he spoke less. But sometimes he caught himself over-sharing. The last thing he wanted was for Mabel to stop liking him. Seeing as she still had a smile on her face whenever he came around, it meant his plan was working. She was starting to like the new him.

"Zach!" Mabel beamed, scurrying out of the house. "You're early."

"Good morning, Mabel. I..."

Before he could finish his sentence, she leaned in and pecked him quickly on the cheek. Zachary bit back a smile as he dropped his head. It was difficult to keep up with the personality he created when Mabel caused his heart to flutter with every single thing that she did.

"Flowers. For you," he managed to say, handing her the wild roses.

"They're beautiful, thank you," she said, taking them from him. They made their way out of the yard, walking side by side. "And I like your hat. You look very nice in that shirt."

"Oh, thank you," he said, blushing. "It's my best shirt."

"Is it?" Mabel giggled. "I see why. It suits you. Did you dress this nicely for me?"

"Well, yes, and no. I have to meet someone important after our stroll. So, I have to dress well. His name is Brandon Post. He's a rancher here in Gray Rock. If I manage to convince him I'm worthy, I might just get another job."

"Another job? Why do you need another job? You don't want to be a miner anymore?"

"No, I'm still a miner, but I figured another source of income isn't a bad idea. It will help a great deal. I'm trying to make my situation better."

"I admire that, Zach. But don't overwork yourself, please. I think being a miner is already hard work. You don't need to add to your stress. Do you think you can handle another job?"

"Yes," he replied. "I have to. But you don't have to trouble yourself with this. Let's change the subject. Let's talk about you. How are you? How're you finding your stay in Gray Rock? I heard you visited the mercantile yesterday with Drusilla."

"I did. We talked a lot about her life before she came here, and my life too. She's really nice to me, and her daughter is just adorable. She keeps saying tree day every chance she gets. Whenever she sees a tree, it's the first thing that comes out of her mouth. When you ask her a question, 'tree day' is always her reply. Drusilla says Jamison is the reason for this. I find it adorable."

"Tree day? That's an odd name for Christmas."

"She can't even pronounce her own name. I'm sure her father used tree day instead because it was easier for her to say. I'm going to remember that so I can use it when we have children."

"I take it you really like children?"

"A great deal," she answered. "They bring so much joy."

"Indeed. I barely see my niece, and yet, I find myself smiling whenever I think of her. Peggy says she looks a lot like me. I find that hard to believe. I mean, it's a girl and she's beautiful. How could she possibly look like ugly, plain-looking me?"

"Oh, stop. You know you're handsome," Mabel said without hesitation. "And it's very possible that she looks like you. It's not particularly about the face. It's the little things. The eyes, nose, shape... she could resemble you in many different ways."

Mabel was saying things but Zachary hadn't gotten past the fact that she called him handsome. He wasn't used to receiving compliments but this one felt really good. Especially since it was coming from someone he really cared about.

"Thank you for the compliment. I think you're really beautiful too."

Mabel blushed. "Thank you. It feels nice hearing you say that."

"I could say the same."

Mabel smiled and nodded. "I really like compliments. I'm telling you this because it's a weakness of mine but I'm letting you in on the secret so that you can use it to your advantage when we get married. If you ever offend me in any way, you can just say something nice to me and I'll forget all about it."

"Oh," he said in response and swallowed. "Okay."

Mabel sighed and dropped the roses to the side. "You're doing it again."

"Doing what?"

"That thing you do. I talk about our future and your mood changes. You stop talking and you keep a straight face. You do it every time. At the mention of marriage, children, or the idea of us living together."

"I didn't realize. I'm sorry."

"No, I don't want you to apologize. I would just like to talk about the prospects of our future without your demeanor changing. I'm not rushing you into anything. I just want to talk about it. To see if we're on the same page? I start to wonder if you want to marry at all."

"I'm sorry... I know I'm awkward." He smiled.

One other thing he liked about Mabel was that she didn't hide the fact that she wanted to settle down with him. She had made up her mind about building a life with him. While the thought thrilled Zachary, it terrified him too. He had to put in more effort if he was ever going to please her. He had to be more than just a miner. Zachary had to make sure that Mabel had no worries in the world. No matter what, and yet, the look on her face made him wonder if he could lose her. What was he doing wrong?

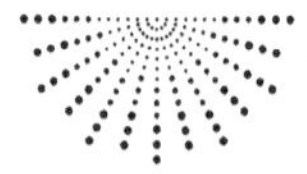

CHAPTER FOURTEEN

Zachary paced outside the ranch, trying to build up the courage he needed to go inside. He knew Brandon Post, but not too well. They only said hello to each other once in a while whenever Zachary passed by his ranch. Ever since Brandon's accident, they had seen less of each other. Zachary wondered if it was ideal to ask Brandon for such a favor. However, Carrie had spoken highly of him, and judging from his brief encounters with the man, Zachary concluded that he would at least give him a listening ear.

Outside the ranch, Brandon appeared to be patting a horse while stealing glances at Olivia, his wife, on the porch. Olivia sat with a letter in her hand and from the look on her face, Zachary could understand why

Brandon was keeping an eye on her. She looked worried as she read through the letter and Brandon looked equally worried for his wife. Seeing the tension between them, Zachary paused, contemplating his next move. Perhaps, the couple needed to talk and he was just going to get in the way and ruin his chances of getting on Brandon's good side.

"Zach?"

Before he could make any decision, Brandon had already seen him and was now gesturing for him to come forward. After taking in a deep breath, Zachary obliged and joined Brandon by the horse.

"Look at you!" Brandon said, chuckling. "Your beard is gone. You look like a completely different person. I almost didn't recognize you at all. You look good."

"Oh, well. I'm starting to like this new look too. Good morning, Brandon," he greeted. "I'm sorry for dropping by like this without any notice. Is this a bad time?"

"No, not at all," Brandon answered.

"Are you sure? I can go and come back some other time," Zach said. "It seems Olivia received some bad news and you both need to talk."

"Oh, it's not bad news," Brandon answered. "I don't know what it is, but if it was bad news, she'd be running here right now, waving the letter in her hand and yelling my name. She's just reading the letter seriously, hence, the look on her face. It's nothing to worry about."

"Oh. You know your wife well," Zachary noted.

"Of course." He smiled. "I heard from Peter that you too just received a bride from West Virginia. I'm happy for you. Congratulations. It's a big step."

"Thank you so much. I really appreciate it."

"I'll give you a small piece of advice," he continued. "Pay attention to little things that your bride does. It really helps. You can buy her flowers, take her on a nice picnic, get her a beautiful dress, and she appreciates all of it. But if you manage to remember what she said three weeks ago about something random, or if you recall the name of her favorite aunt growing up... you might just make her cry happy tears. It's the little things that matter the most. Wives love husbands that listen to them."

Zachary nodded and smiled. "My bride likes compliments. And my hat."

"Oh, really?" Brandon chuckled. "That's a start. It's good you remember. Keep it up."

"I'll be sure to. We're still getting to know each other, and I'm sure that when I've settled into my new self, we'll get married and start our family."

"Your new self?"

"Oh, it's just..." Zachary laughed awkwardly. "You know me, Brandon. I'm not this calm or collected. I changed my look, so I figured I'd change how I talk and how I act so I can be a better person. Like Mabel deserves."

"That's sweet of you. Just don't change too much. You want your bride to recognize the man she came this far to meet; she might like him over this new you."

"I won't. But it's sort of the reason I came here to see you in the first place," Zachary continued. "I was wondering if you need any form of help on the ranch. I'm looking for work and if I do right by you, I was hoping to earn a stake in the ranch over time. Or at least earn enough to buy land of my own."

Brandon listened to him, nodding his head. As they talked, Olivia walked up to them still holding the letter in her hand. She greeted Zachary before leaning into her husband's embrace.

"Are you all right?" Brandon asked her, caressing her arm.

Olivia nodded. "I am. It's nothing serious. It's a letter from a friend."

"Something I should be worried about?"

"Well, we'll talk about it later," she answered. "It's something that bothers me a bit, but I have a solution to it, so I don't think I need to worry. You can read it when we get inside."

"All right," he answered, placing a peck on her forehead. "Zachary is here seeking work. You know how we were talking about Willow County and how we were going to get those horses?"

"Yes. It's perfect," Olivia said. "It works."

Zachary watched them speak between themselves and he could pick out one or two things. It seemed like he appeared at the right time when they were looking for someone to help with the horses. They spoke of Willow County, two towns from Gray Rock, and about purchasing some horses. Zachary straightened his back, ready to convince them that he was indeed the man for whatever job it was that they had for him.

"Zach, right now I have this issue with some of the horse wranglers I used to work with," Brandon started. "You know I have this injury from my accident that left me with a limp?"

"Of course. At some point, it was all the miners talked about. I couldn't see why it was funny, or important to them. I mean, it was just an accident."

"Well, they talked about it a lot because they used to tease him for it," Olivia explained. "They made it some sort of routine to seek him out every day to make fun of him for it. Brandon always ignored them, and eventually, they went away."

"Well, that's not really what happened. You chased them away with your anger. That's why they left," Brandon corrected her.

"I had my fair share of their teasing when I was younger," Zachary revealed. "It's weird how some of them still work there at the mine with me. I started working at the mine at a young age, so they used to tease me a lot and push me around. At one point when I was almost twenty, I had grown quite a lot, and I was taller than most of them. I stood up for myself and told them to stop or I'd make them. Since then, they mostly ignored me."

Brandon and Olivia exchanged looks and smiled. "That's good to hear," Brandon said. "In fact, it's what we need."

Zachary arched his eyebrows. "How do you mean?"

"I need to purchase some horses from Willow County. Usually, I'd go myself, but I found out that as of late, these men tend to look down on me because of my injury. While I don't particularly care what they say, I do need new horses and they're not acting particularly nice. Will you be interested in making the journey to Willow County and purchasing these horses at a good price? You don't seem like the kind of man they can walk over. I know it's almost Christmas and it's all right to say no, but it's the only work I have right now, and it pays well. You'll get a cut for every purchase you make and I'll employ you to work on the ranch after that."

"You really think I'm the man for this job?" he asked, bringing both hands to his hips.

"Have you worked with horses before?" Brandon inquired.

"Yes, sir, I have."

"Then I think you're the man for the job. I'll just tell you one or two things to say, and how you should bargain with them. The rest is easy."

"All I have to do is convince them to sell to you?" Zachary asked. "That doesn't sound so hard."

"I'm hoping they'd look at a strong man like yourself and not give you any problems. Don't worry. As I said, it's easy. You just need to stand your ground."

It was a good job. Plus, it sounded easy too. What bothered Zachary was the fact that he might need his rough, former self to bargain with men that rarely listened to reasoning. But it was something he was willing to do as long as he could earn some more money.

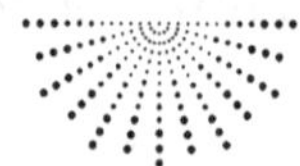

CHAPTER FIFTEEN

The sun had left a red glow on the horizon, and there were signs that it was about to snow. On his way home, Zachary ran into Peter, who was on his way to the mercantile. Zachary decided to go with him instead of going straight home to spend the rest of the night alone. He was in a good mood, after securing the job at Brandon Post's ranch. All he wanted to do was share his good news with as many people as he could before he had to leave.

"You say you're leaving tomorrow?" Peter asked him. "Isn't that too soon?"

"Brandon said I can leave for Willow County whenever I wanted, so I told him I can go tomorrow. It'll give me enough time to settle the deal with the horse wranglers and convince them to sell on Brandon's terms."

"Are you sure you can do it?" Peter asked. "These wranglers are not the best of people. I don't know what's wrong with them but there have been some stories."

Zachary scoffed. "I'll get it done. You're forgetting that I'm not usually like this. I can be intimidating if I want to be. I could put this act aside and be the tough and rough around the edges kind of man that gets the job done. It's who I was all my life."

"Act?" Peter asked. "What do you mean act?"

"Not, not act. What I mean is, I can go back to being my former self. The bearded man with dirty hands that no one liked to cross because of my look, my build, and my demeanor. I stopped being that person the moment I cut off my beard, and my hair and put on that suit. Now, I'm just a sweet regular man that has a bride who likes him a great deal. And I'm proud of that."

Peter paused in his tracks. "Zach, this sweet, regular man. Was he the person you introduced to Mabel?"

Zachary's eyebrows furrowed. "What do you mean?"

"In the letter where you fully introduced yourself to Mabel. How did you describe yourself?"

"Well, I was honest. I admitted to her that I was a bit rough around the edges, but I like to be expressive with my feelings and I always stand up for myself no matter what. I told her I was an open person, and that I was willing to do anything to make my family comfortable."

"Zach, don't you think you're much too different from that person right now?"

'I'm not understanding you." Zachary shook his head.

Peter placed a hand on his shoulder and sighed. "Maybe we shouldn't have cut your hair. I'm afraid we might have let go of the real Zachary Warner too," he teased.

Zachary rolled his eyes and chuckled. "He's right here. He's just going through some changes to make sure that he's the perfect gentleman for his lovely bride."

"Did you ask your lovely bride if she wanted a gentleman, or if she wanted the Zach that was 'rough around the edges'? When we asked you to clean up, it was so that you gave a good first impression. You should be yourself with Mabel. Be free. I still think you need to wait a bit and spend Christmas with Mabel before you leave. You'll be gone for the holiday."

"Oh, no. I'll be back right on time. I won't miss the opportunity to watch the snow at night with Mabel. It's what she wants, and it's what I want too. I was thinking of preparing a small picnic for her outside while we watch it snow. I figured it would be romantic."

"Sure. But you might freeze to death," Peter revealed. "That won't be very fun."

"You're right. A nice dinner by the window will have to do."

"How about you ask her what she wants to do and not just assume?"

"Mabel wants to get married. Since I can't do that for her yet, I have to make up for it somehow."

"Why can't you do that for her? I thought you wanted to be married by Christmas?"

"I thought I'd be ready. But I'm not. I'm still trying to buy land. I need to make sure she has a good place to stay."

"What if she doesn't care about these things and all she wants is to be by your side while you both figure things out. From the look of things, it seems like you're handling everything all on your own. That's not how a marriage works. It's like a partnership. Equal rights."

"All right, now you're just assuming."

"You're doing the same thing too."

"I'm doing the right thing."

"I don't think so."

"What are you two bickering about?"

Wyatt met them at the entrance of the mercantile, just as they were about to go inside.

"Hello, Wyatt," Peter said to him. "Zach here is planning on leaving Gray Rock a week before Christmas on business. Please tell him it's not a good idea. He should spend the time here instead with his bride."

Wyatt glanced at the entrance. "Speaking of brides-"

"It's a good opportunity for me, Wyatt," Zachary spoke, cutting him off. "Tell Peter he's overreacting. I'll be back long before Christmas day. Brandon is giving me a chance to work for him. He wants me to go to Willow County and purchase some horses for his ranch. It's a great way to make some extra money."

"You're leaving Gray Rock?"

Mabel's voice caused Zachary to shudder. He lifted his head and found her standing behind Wyatt with a dejected look on her face. Drusilla was standing by her side with baby Carolyn in her arms. Zachary swallowed. He had planned on telling her the good news the next day before he left.

"I tried to tell you," Wyatt whispered.

Zachary turned to her. "Yes, Mabel. On business."

"Why don't we give them room to talk," Peter suggested.

Now alone, Zachary stood in front of Mabel with his eyes fixated on the ground. It was a good thing for both of them, but he felt guilty for some reason. He didn't want to leave her. Even though she had people to keep her company, Zachary preferred to be by her side.

It's all for her... you're doing this for her.

"Are you really leaving, Zach?" she asked again.

"Only for a few days."

"It's almost Christmas. We had plans to decorate a tree and to watch it snow that day, together... while we talked all through the night."

"And we will do all of that," he assured her. "I just need to make a quick trip to Willow County and I'll be back before you know it. This will be good for us."

"It won't be good for me. What trip? What business?"

"I just need to negotiate the price of the horses with some wranglers and once they agree to Brandon's terms, I'll be back."

"Zach, in the letter you sent me, you introduced yourself as a local miner to me. Not a horse wrangler or a businessman. Now, I'm not saying you cannot pursue greener pastures, but we haven't even gotten married yet and I've been here for almost a month. Don't you want to marry me? Are you having doubts?"

"Of course not."

"Then we're supposed to be doing all of this together. You're supposed to talk to me about things that are troubling you, or decisions that you make. I've been led to believe that is how a relationship works. But you're acting all alone and I can't tell what you're thinking."

"Mabel," Zachary stuttered. "I'm just trying to be the man that you deserve the most. An honorable man that has his act together. I want to give that to you before we proceed."

"I'm not asking for anything."

"You don't have to ask, it's my duty to give it to you. Don't you want a good and comfortable life?"

"I want a husband. I want to marry the man that wrote to me, telling me he was seeking a wife to build a life with. I don't want an already established man. You're pushing me away, Zach, and I don't appreciate it. Every time we meet and I bring up talks of marriage, you tense up and change the subject. It makes me wonder if I made the right decision coming here in the first place."

"Mabel, please see things from my perspective," he asked.

"And you sound nothing like you did in the letters," she continued. "It's like I'm looking and talking to a different person. Sometimes, I see the Zach that I had read about, and other times, I fear I just imagined him."

"I'm doing all of this for you."

"And I'm telling you that I don't want you to. It'll become a burden on me if you make the decision solely based on what you think I would want rather than talking to me about it."

"Mabel," he said, placing both hands on her shoulders. "I'll be back soon. I promise we'll talk then. I'll have some money and we can both..."

"It's not about the money. It's the fact that Carrie and Drusilla... even Sheriff Hill all seem excited about us getting married, but you don't. It's the only thing that takes your smile away. I need to think, Zach. You can go get the horses you want to get so badly, and when you return, we need to talk about us and where this is going. I really like you a lot, and I know that you like me too, but it's not enough. If we're not on the same page, then I don't think we should drag this on any longer."

Without allowing him to speak, Mabel walked away with her head down. He had tried so hard to avoid hurting her with his actions, but he failed. Now, Mabel was unsure of his intentions toward her and he wondered if the marriage was ever going to happen.

Was he ever going to convince himself that he was man enough to be with a woman like Mabel forever?

CHAPTER SIXTEEN

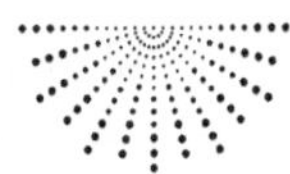

It had been two days since Zachary left for Willow County. The last time Mabel saw him was at the mercantile when they argued about their relationship. Mabel had not stopped thinking about their conversation ever since. She didn't know what to make of it. Zachary never seemed to listen to how she felt. It was becoming frustrating and as each day went by she felt more and more alone. Did he care for her at all?

He was aware she wanted to marry him, but he was actively shunning the conversation. Each time he avoided it her confidence took a dive and soon she knew she would have to make a decision; did she talk to Carrie about finding her a different match?

This had to work, for Mabel had no other plan for her life. When she arrived in Gray Rock filled with hope for her future, she never imagined she'd be in this position. She found herself questioning his intentions. Was it all a lie? Or was there something about her that he didn't like?

"You're staring at my belly like it has two heads," Amy said, snapping Mabel out of her thoughts.

She had not realized that she was still staring at Amy's stomach. Embarrassed, Mabel looked away quickly. She and Amy had formed a friendship in the past couple of days. At first, Mabel used to accompany Drusilla to visit pregnant Amy and help her with chores around the house, but in the past two days, Mabel found her way to Amy's house by herself. Drusilla and Gloria had gone to the mercantile to do some last-minute shopping before Christmas, so with nothing to do, Mabel decided to spend the day helping Amy.

"You like children, don't you?" Amy asked her, adjusting her eyeglasses.

"I love them. Hopefully, I'll have some of my own. The more the merrier." A wistful smile came over her face, would this ever happen?

"You and Zachary are going to make beautiful children. I know this for a fact. You're a beautiful woman, and he's good-looking too. Your home will be filled with laughter."

Mabel sighed and fiddled with her fingers. "Hopefully. I want that more than anything. But I can't help but think that he doesn't want the same. At least not yet. I wonder if I should have come to Gray Rock in the first place... I wouldn't have done so... if he hadn't written to me saying that he was ready to marry. I thought he was ready, I thought he was serious. That's why I came here in the first place."

"What's the issue?" Amy asked, sitting up. "Did you two argue?"

"Not really. I just told Zach that I didn't understand what he was doing. It was just before he went away... I don't know if I ruined things between us by saying all of that." She sighed and shrugged her shoulders.

"What is the problem?" Amy asked.

"He's sending me mixed signals, Amy. One minute he smiles and we talk for hours on end, then the next, he's quiet and cold. It's like he catches himself doing something he's not supposed to be doing, so he reins it in.

That's what I feel and I told him that I need to know what is happening."

"You want certainty, and Zach isn't giving you this?"

"Exactly. It's all right if he isn't ready to get married right now. I just want to know that he wants to. I think he's just using the house and job as an excuse to push me away because if he really wanted to marry me, he would. Regardless. I've told him many times that it doesn't matter to me, but I think it matters to him. So much so that he isn't ready to get married unless he achieves what he wants to achieve. If he wasn't ready, he should have told me from the start."

Amy sighed as she rubbed her stomach and then eased her back. "It's all right that you have worries. Before I became pregnant I was this emotional mess that no one could help."

Mabel chuckled. "Emotional mess?"

"I'm not kidding. After I lost the first baby, I became a shadow of who I was. I would cry a lot, push everyone away, blame myself, and blame everyone. I wouldn't eat, and I would cry myself to sleep... for months on end. I wonder how Peter was able to put up with me. But everything worked out in the end. I realized that I needed him, as much as he needed me. I got pregnant again, and we've been just fine since then. If anyone had told me back then, when I was practically drowning in my own tears, that I would be this happy now, I would have probably screamed at them. But look. Things turned out fine. They always do."

"Do you think I have nothing to worry about?" Mabel asked.

"I think it's all right to worry. But don't let it weigh you down. Things happen, and there will be obstacles, but in the end, what's yours will find you. Peter was supposed to marry Gloria not me at the start. Did you know this?"

"No." Mabel shook her head. "How did that happen?"

"She was his first match, but one of her letters got damaged, they wanted different things. They weren't meant to be even though Peter was willing to look past the obstacles in their path, it just wasn't meant to be. We were meant to be. We knew from the start. I had a lot of insecurities, but he never failed to reassure me that I was enough. I feel safe with him. It all worked out for good. Gloria is happy, we're happy... you'll be fine. Just let things play out. You have no control over it anyway."

"You know what? You're right, Amy. I'm here, I'm not leaving. I'll figure this out. Something has to work. First, I need to figure out where Zach stands and we'll go from there. It still feels like he's holding things back from me, and I'm going to find out what it is."

"Good. That's the spirit."

Mabel squeezed Amy's hand. "Thank you, Amy."

"You're welcome."

They spent the rest of the day talking about Christmas. Amy was hoping she'd have her baby before then, so she could spend Christmas day with her little one in her arms. Mabel was trying her best to listen but all she could think of was Zachary. When was he returning? Was he angry with her for demanding more from him? Had he changed his mind about the whole thing? What was she going to do?

CHAPTER SEVENTEEN

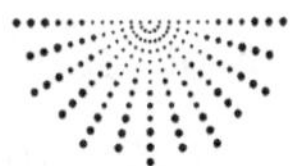

"Well, we ain't addin' a penny more. Take it, or we'll take our business elsewhere," Zach said. "I ain't got any more time to waste here."

The negotiations were taking longer than Zachary had hoped they would. The horsemen were refusing to budge and the fee they had suggested was extortionate. Zach had made the decision to drop the gentle personality he had created for himself to impress Mabel. It was better if he talked to these men in his normal, strict tone and met them on equal grounds. These horsemen were known to take advantage of people at whatever chance they got. They were discussing money; hence, it was only ideal that they let their guard up. But Zachary wasn't planning on backing down either.

"We're the best in the West. No one will sell such good stock to you."

"We'll see." Zachary smiled. "We're talking about Brandon Post. He's a big player in Gray Rock, and soon, in the entire West. You can either sell at a reasonable price now... or you don't. In the end, it ain't gonna be my loss. It'll be yours. Once he signs this deal with the men that traveled all the way from California to speak to him, you ain't gonna stand a chance. I promise you'd be selling for way less."

The three men exchanged a look and whispered amongst themselves. Zachary kept on his best poker face. He knew they were inflating their prices because Brandon had a limp. They saw him as less of a man and were taking advantage of him. He had no idea if it was possible to source the horses elsewhere, but he figured the best way to get these varmints to sit down and negotiate, without them looking down on Brandon, would be to make them think they were missing out on an opportunity.

These men had the best horses in Willow County, and Brandon wanted them... but he needed them at a fair price. Zachary was willing to play all the cards at his disposal. He had already fallen back to his former, rougher patterns of speech. Nothing was stopping him from taking it a step further if the need ever came. These guys had been known to rough up a customer to make sure they got what they wanted. Well, they could try, he was ready.

"I think he's lying," Zachary heard one of the men whisper. "We ain't selling to Brandon Post on these terms. The man can't even ride a horse anymore with that injury of his. No one's gonna sell to him."

"Maybe we should just take the money and leave him with the dregs," one of the men said.

They had shown Zachary several old horses that were ready for pasture, they certainly couldn't do a day's work. They wanted too much even for those. Now they were talking about stealing from him. It was time to step things up a little. "I can ride a horse," Zachary said, glaring at them for insulting Brandon. There was just no need for it, besides, Brandon could ride now and he rode well and no one was stealing his money. "I'm also here as Brandon's negotiator. This means insulting him, is insulting me and I don't take kindly to you insulting my boss... or threatening to take his money. I could show you how I ride horses if you want. But sometimes, my horse fails to see insolent horsemen in its path and it might just trample over you."

"Are you threatening me?" the man questioned.

Zachary scoffed and took a step forward, looking down at the man. "I don't make threats. I take action. Now, are you sellin' or not because it's Christmas Eve and I ain't wastin' my time here anymore. We've been negotiatin' for three whole days. I'm done. Tell me what your decision is, and I advise that you state it, without speakin' on Brandon's injury, or else my fist might end up in your face."

"Look," the first horseman said, stepping forward. "We would sell to you, but we want more money."

"You're in Willow County. This is the best price you'll get from any rancher or horseman lookin' to buy this season. Once it's Christmas, no one will come to you askin' about horses. This is a fair price, a good price, and the price you sold to another rancher just two days ago. I know you have just put the price up because you think Brandon is easy prey, well, he ain't. Sell to me now, or you will be left tending to these horses till March and by then, the price would have dropped, and Brandon would still have his horses because you ain't the only horsemen looking to sell. You're just the closest ones. Do you understand what I'm sayin' to you?"

The man stepped back and cleared his throat. "I mean, it's business. You ain't gotta be all feisty during negotiations. We're just talkin' here."

"I don't talk for this long, and when I do, I get cranky. Now, tell me. Are you selling or not? I want your answer to be the first thing that comes out of that mouth. No more back and forth."

Zachary was pleased, knowing that he had riled them up enough to make them question their stance. They were only inflating the price because they wanted to ride Brandon Post. Little did they know that Zachary was coming in his stead.

"Fine. We'll be in Gray Rock shortly to finalize the details of the deal," the man finally said, succumbing to Zachary's will.

"Thank you, gentlemen. We look forward to receiving these horses today. Any more than that, and the deal is off. I'll see you in Gray Rock."

Without hesitation, Zachary mounted his horse and made his way for Gray Rock as fast as he could. He almost had to spend Christmas day in Willow County because of the stubborn horsemen. Mabel would have never forgiven him for it. Now that he had secured the deal, he eagerly rode home, happy that he could prove his worth to Brandon and prove his commitment to Mabel.

If she still wanted him. Her words had been in his head ever since he left.

CHAPTER EIGHTEEN

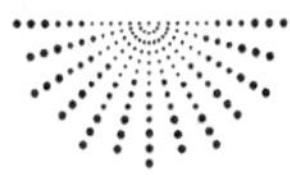

There was a proud smile slapped across Zachary's face as he watched Brandon shake hands with the horse wranglers. He stood with his hands on his hips, watching the deal that he had made happen by being his true self. It was certain that not everyone fancied a man who used his build to ensure that people did the right thing, but that was who Zachary really was. He had tried over time not to be that person anymore so he didn't attract a lot of attention to himself, but what if that was the person Mabel needed? What if the act he was putting on was of no use? What if he was pushing her away without knowing it?

"Zach, we got the horses," Brandon said to him, gesturing for him to come over.

"Congratulations," Zachary said. "And congratulations to you too, gentlemen. You made a wise choice."

"I mean, ain't it baffling that Mr. Post is so keen on acquirin' more horses when he can't even ride," the first horseman said. "I mean, come on. Don't y'all find it a little bit absurd?"

"There ain't nothing absurd about a horseman acquirin' more horses," Zachary responded in his stead. "And you better watch your mouth now. You have no right to mock him. I don't think you want to be talkin' back to the man that's about to pay you for your horses. If you keep refusin' to show some respect, I might have to make you."

Zachary curled his fingers into a fist and stood in front of Brandon, squaring up against the wranglers. They were stubborn men who rarely listened and were still bitter about the fact that they couldn't milk more money out of Brandon even when he was the one offering the most. And Zachary had no doubt that if they thought they could get away with it that they would have taken the money and left him beaten on the ground. Well, not today gents, he was on top of it.

"All right now, there's no need for threats," the horseman said. "I merely asked a question."

"Don't ask stupid questions like that again," Zachary warned them. "Now, get your money and leave. It was nice doing business with you."

Zachary left them to tend to the newly acquired horses while Brandon made the deal. Once the men left, Brandon walked over to his side and smiled at him without saying anything.

"What?" Zachary asked. "You're proud of me, aren't you?"

"Very," Brandon answered, chuckling. "Usually, I wouldn't respond to them. They refuse to sell? Fine. I offer the most money, and I can take my business some-where else. But I really wanted this stallion and these mares, and you got them for me. Thank you for your show of strength. The wranglers will know not to mess with me now."

"They don't deserve to be paid that much, Brandon. They don't deserve a penny of your money. You should look for other people to do business with. Not these ones that prey on your weakness and try to use it to their advantage. You know what they said to me when I first arrived? They said 'they'd much rather sell to horsemen that will take proper care of the horses, not one that's missing a leg.' I mean, it's business, what does it matter?"

"It doesn't matter. As you said, they try to use my weakness to their advantage. They hoped that their words would get to me so I would offer more. I'm a businessman. I'm not a fool and I definitely won't fall for their tricks."

"Well, as long as you're happy with the sale, then all is good."

Brandon placed a hand on Zachary's shoulder and squeezed. "I am pleased. Very pleased. You work here at the ranch now and don't worry about your payment. I'll have it ready for you at the end of the day. You're practically the strongest man I know. I'm sure Mabel is happy she has you. She won't have any worries in the world with you by her side. It can be rough out here, the miners can be cruel, but with you by her side, she will be safe. No one can mess with her."

Zachary arched his eyebrows. "You think she'd prefer this side of me, to a much gentler man?"

"A gentler man? You can be gentle with her in private. But I think most women would prefer a man they can rely on. A real man."

"But you're gentle, Brandon. You barely talk, and you never respond to the people that try to talk down on you.

Does Olivia complain that you're too gentle?"

"Of course not. I can take whatever these bullies throw at me. I don't care. I have a limp, so what? I can still ride, and it's all thanks to Olivia. I might stay quiet most of the time, but when it comes to my wife, I'll be whatever she needs me to be. For instance, I would take you on in a fight if you ever disrespected her. She knows this. That's the assurance she needs and I've given it to her. I don't play, or remain quiet when it comes to my wife."

Zachary stopped to think. Not once had he reassured Mabel of anything since she arrived in Gray Rock. All he had told her was that he was only going to marry her once he got a suitable place for them to stay. What if Mabel needed more reassurance than that? Perhaps that was the reason she had been so upset.

"Peter? Peter!" Zachary heard Brandon call out to them.

Peter had a worried look on his face as he and Carl, the sheriff ran into the ranch.

"What's the matter?" Brandon asked. "Why do you both look so worried?"

"Amy's in labor," Peter revealed. "We can't find the doctor or the midwife. I don't know what to do at this point."

CHAPTER NINETEEN

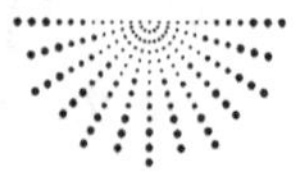

"Try to breathe, Amy. Don't panic. Everything is going to be all right," Mabel said but the fear in her heart said anything but.

Mabel felt sorry for Amy. The labor seemed hard and no one was coming, what could they do?

In some ways, Amy was relieved, for it had been 3 weeks over what they thought was the due date. Of course, these things were never very accurate, but with losing one baby, Amy was especially worried.

The labor had been hard so far. Amy's waters broke and dropped her to her knees. Mabel had helped her to her bed and then ran for help. But where was the midwife or the doctor, who was going to help them?

Mabel feared for Amy. She seemed to be in a lot of pain, and given the fact that she had lost a child before, Amy was panicking.

"It's all right. I promise you. It's all going to be all right," Mabel tried to reassure her. "Just breathe and help will be here soon."

Carrie wiped Amy's head with a cloth, trying to calm her down. "You'll be fine. Just take deep breaths. The doctor will be here soon. Carl and Peter have gone to fetch him."

"Oh, it hurts, Carrie. It hurts a lot," Amy groaned. "I think the baby needs to come out now. I don't think I'll have the strength to push later on"

"You can't push now until there's someone here to deliver the baby," Carrie told her, for she had seen that something was wrong. "We have to be careful this time. Just hold on for a bit, I'm sure Peter is on his way back."

"Why aren't they back yet?" she groaned again. "They've been gone for so long. What if something happened to them? Remember the time when Peter went to the center of the town to pick up Drusilla and he got accosted by that gang and they beat him up? What if?"

"Amy!" Carrie cautioned her. "Stop imagining the worst and causing yourself to panic. Besides, he's with Carl, the sheriff, remember? Relax. They're on their way back, I'm sure of it."

"Just try and relax," Mabel chimed in. "Think of the baby. The baby needs you to relax. If you're agitated like this, then the baby is agitated too. We don't want anything to happen to the baby. Soon, the doctor will arrive, and you'll have a smooth delivery."

"I can't," Amy began to sob. "Oh, what if something happens to me this time? What if I'm the one that dies? I'm getting tired, Mabel. I'm trying, but I'm in too much pain."

"The pain will subside with time," Carrie told her. "It's coming at intervals, that's normal."

"Yes, but they aren't far apart," she answered. "That's because the baby is ready to come out. Now, the pain itself won't kill you, but if you decided to let it win, if you decide to let it tire you out, then you won't be able to push. If you don't push, then the baby will be in danger. So, when the pain comes, just wait for it to pass and it will. You're not going to die. Drusilla had a safe delivery, Gloria had a safe delivery, and you will too. All right? You're lucky you're giving birth on Christmas Eve.

There's something called a Christmas miracle, you know?"

Carrie's words seemed to resonate with Amy. She mellowed and laid back down on the bed, breathing rapidly through her mouth. Mabel held Amy's hand in hers and whispered to her, telling her everything was going to be all right.

"They're here," Carrie said, rising to her feet at the same time Peter, Carl, and Zachary walked into the room. "Where's the doctor?"

"He's not in," Carl answered. "We can't find the midwife either."

"Oh, dear Lord, help me." Amy began to pant. "Oh, what's going to happen to me?"

"Try to relax, Amy," Carl told her. "I will go back out and keep searching everywhere for the doctor. I assure you that I'll find him soon. But in the meantime, Zachary says he can help."

While they were talking, Zachary was busy folding up his sleeves. He didn't spare Mabel a glance but she understood why. Amy was important at the moment and if he could help then it would mean a great deal.

"I can help," Zachary said. "Trust me, Amy. I helped my sister give birth to her child, and I've done it with horses too. It was just the both of us and I got instructions from a midwife on how to help her. The baby was born safe and sound. I'll make sure yours is too."

"That's what you meant when you said you helped your sister a great deal when you lived together?" Carrie asked him.

Zachary nodded. "It was. Now, I'll need clean water, some soap, a towel, some warm water too, and alcohol if you have any."

"I'll get them," Peter said and quickly exited the room.

"All right," Zach whispered. "Amy? Are you listening to me?"

"Yes?" she answered in a quivering voice.

"It's all right to be scared. In fact, I'd think you were weird if you weren't. When my sister was giving birth she cried at first, but when she started pushing, she forgot about her tears. At some point, your instincts will kick in and you'll want to push. All I ask is that when it does, you'll give it all you've got. I'll tell you when to stop pushing so I can guide the baby out by hand once I see the head."

Amy exhaled calmly to steady her breathing. "I'll do as you say."

"Just trust him," Mabel said, holding Amy's hands tightly. "This is the moment you've been waiting for. Give it your best shot."

CHAPTER TWENTY

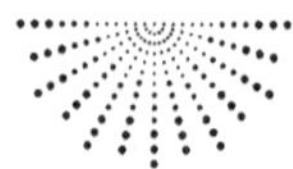

The labor was hard, the baby needed turning, but Zachary stayed calm and professional and handled it as if he had done it a thousand times.

The sound of a baby's cry filled the room. "It's a boy!"

Zachary's announcement caused Peter to fall to his knees and Amy to cry happy tears. Mabel watched him with wide eyes as he wrapped the screaming baby in a towel and handed him to Carrie who then placed the baby in Amy's arms.

Zachary cleaned his hands in the water and toweled himself, all the time staring at the miracle that he had just delivered.

"Congratulations, Amy. I'm happy for you," Mabel said.

"Thank you, Mabel," Amy sobbed.

Mabel quietly left her side so Peter could hold his wife and his new child in his arms. Carrie started cleaning up with a wide grin on her face. Mabel tried not to look at Zachary because there were tears in her eyes, and she didn't want him to see her like that. But then she felt a hand reach for hers and as she turned to look at him, Zachary led her out of the room down the stairs, and to the porch.

"I'm fine," Mabel protested. "It's just a happy moment."

"I know," he answered before pulling her into a hug. He rocked her from side to side, patting her on the back. "I missed you."

"I missed you too," she whispered and sniffed back the tears. "So, how was your trip to Willow County?"

"Fruitful," he answered. "I secured the deal. Brandon got his horses and I get to work at the ranch. I can provide for both of us now. You don't need to worry about anything."

Mabel sighed and took Zachary's hand into hers. "It's still snowing. Can we go for a walk? I miss our walks."

"Sure, let's go."

Hand in hand, they walked out into the yard. Mabel watched her feet sink into the freshly falling snow as she walked. She had questions for Zachary but had no idea where to start from. Still, this was the moment to clear the air between them.

"Zach-"

"You look really beautiful today," he said, cutting her off.

Mabel started to smile before she realized that he was trying to use her weakness against her. "No, don't do that."

"I really like your long hair."

"Stop." She giggled. "I'm not angry at you. At least not anymore. What you did in there was really amazing. You should be proud of yourself."

"Thank you," he said.

"But we need to talk about us, Zach-"

"I know what you're about to say, Mabel," he said, cutting her off. Zach stopped in his tracks and took both her hands into his. "I want to be honest about something with you. I don't know how you will react, but I've been thinking about what Peter said to me the day before I left for Willow County. He said I didn't ask you before I decided to change my personality to please you. He said, marriage was a partnership, and it was equal rights. He said I had to talk to you about everything. No matter how little."

"He's right," Mabel said, almost in a whisper.

"I didn't plan this, Mabel," he started. "I had decided to be myself when I met you, but that changed the minute I laid eyes on you. Before you came to Gray Rock, I had really messy long hair and a full face of beard. I didn't pay much attention to my looks. Ever. But people around me told me that I needed to clean up and look nice for you. So, I took their advice and cleaned up. I shaved, and Peter offered me a suit, and I was thrilled by it. When I saw you, I was so glad I cleaned up. My look that particular day gave me an idea. I decided to be formal. Reserved. Like a gentleman. I thought ladies loved gentlemen. But I don't think you do. Because the more I act that way, the more confused you get."

Mabel nodded. "Now, I understand. It was the suit too, for me. You reminded me of someone the first day we met. Back in West Virginia, my uncle wanted me to marry a banker named Edgar. He is a terrible person and he is one of the reasons I left. You dressed exactly like him when you came to pick me up. I was taken aback. I mean, you said you were a miner. But you didn't dress like a miner. I know miners have dirty hands; they sometimes look rough because of all the work they do. I was prepared to see you like that. I didn't care. I already liked you before I even saw you. I still don't know how that's possible. Your advert in the paper was like a saving grace for me. There were others, but I was drawn to yours. I knew I really liked you when you talked to me at dinner that day about your parents. You seemed so... vulnerable. But you immediately closed up after that."

Zachary sighed. "Mabel, I am far from the fine man I try to portray. I don't wear hats all the time, or white shirts. My hands are dirty most of the time because sometimes I forget to wash them when I return from the mine. Sometimes, I'm too tired to clean up after a long day of working so I go straight to bed. It's funny how I never did that when Peggy was around. I live in a rented room near the mercantile. It's small, and I'm ashamed to let you see it. I am a ragged orphan and all I want is someone special to share my life with. I'm sorry if you wanted more, and I haven't been able to give it to you. That's why I've been trying so hard to get more work. I didn't think I deserved you, so I tried to change who I was. I'm sorry. I'm not a man of few words. I talk a lot. Some of the miners find it annoying. I hardly dress nicely, and I only recently learned how to talk like this to fit in."

Mabel giggled and cupped his cheeks. "You silly man. I didn't come all the way to the West to find a boring, quiet man. I came to find a strong man. A fighter. A real man, with a sensitive soul. I do tend to talk a lot too."

"That's a good thing," he said, chuckling. "We have that in common. I'm sorry about confusing you. Yes, I do want to get married to you and start our life together. I'm sure of it. But all I ask is for some time to get us a place to stay first. It won't take long. I just want to have a decent place for you to stay after we get married. I promise I won't keep you in the dark about anything. We'll do it together. I've saved up enough money now, and soon we'll have our wedding."

Mabel placed a peck on his cheek. "Together. That's all I wanted."

Zachary responded to her peck by placing a kiss on her lips. He then pulled her into a hug and they remained like that, basking in the warmth of the embrace.

"You know, I couldn't take my eyes off of you in there," Mabel revealed. "You looked so serious. Like you knew exactly what you were doing. It was so nice to watch you help someone like that."

"I was trying so hard not to look at you," he answered. "I didn't want to get distracted."

"I noticed. I'm happy you were able to help Amy. I don't even want to imagine what might have happened if you weren't here. I like how you were able to calm Amy down too. Carrie and I tried but she wouldn't relax. You're good with people. That's a nice thing. I've only been here a little over a month and I've experienced so many different things and feelings. Before today, I had never watched a woman give birth. It was so fascinating and I can't wait to write to Greta about it."

"What about your uncle?" he asked. "Have you heard anything from him?"

"No," she replied. "Nothing yet. I'll ask Greta in my next letter, but I think he has already left town to start his new life somewhere else. I can't explain what I always feel whenever I think of the fact that I may never see him again."

Zachary caressed her back. "Even though he was a bad uncle to you, you're going to miss him. He's the only living blood relative that you know. But you don't have to worry about anything. I'm your family now. I'll be anything you want me to be. Just trust me. We'll build our life together, have kids, and start our own family. I'll work hard to make sure we don't lack for anything we need, and we'll always have the most wonderful Christmas celebrations every year."

"We'll have family traditions too," she said. "Greta's family have this tradition they do where all the children are in charge of cooking dinner for the whole family. It happens twice a month. They always mess up the recipes but her parents eat whatever they put on the table and claim that it's delicious even when it's not. Greta says it's one of the reasons she loves her parents so much. I want traditions like that too."

"And we'll have them. We'll even come up with better ones."

Mabel reached up on her tiptoes and kissed him again. Amy was right. Things always had a way of working themselves out. Mabel had no reason to worry in the first place.

CHAPTER TWENTY-ONE

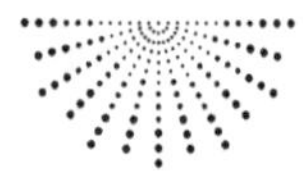

"Your baby is so beautiful, Amy. Congratulations and Merry Christmas," Mabel said.

It was Christmas morning, and it was a full house. Every one of Carrie's couples was present. Everyone came with a gift for the baby. Everyone except Zachary and Mabel. Apparently, they were all aware that Amy was going to put to bed around Christmas, so they had prepared gifts pending the time she had the baby. Since Zachary and Mabel were relatively new to the party, and since they had only recently started the relationship all over, they had not thought of it. Peter told them that it didn't matter, but Zachary had already discussed with Mabel that they were getting the baby a shawl after Christmas.

"Thank you all for deciding to spend such a special holiday here with us," Peter said, holding a bottle of wine. "I cannot even explain how happy I am right now. I'm overjoyed and overwhelmed with love and peace. Amy, I want to thank you, especially, for carrying our child and being such a strong woman. I know it wasn't easy."

Zachary pulled Mabel into his embrace and stroked her arm. They had remained in Peter's home and talked all through the night, watching the snow fall as they snuggled underneath a big blanket. They had only attempted to sleep when the sun was starting to rise, but they hadn't shut their eyes for long before guests started to arrive. It was the first time in his entire life that Zachary had done such a thing. It felt good, and he looked forwards to more days like that, listening to Mabel talk.

Once everyone had a glass in their hand, Peter shared the bottle of wine with everyone except Amy and raised his glass. "A toast to Christmas, to my beautiful wife, to my Christmas miracle, our son, although I don't know what to name him yet. I'd like to also toast to this family of friends, and to many more happy memories. Finally, a toast to Zachary Warner. You're a good friend, Zach, and I am so happy that you were there for Amy. I commend your efforts and we will never forget them. Thank you. And thank you all. Merry Christmas!"

They all drank and Zachary watched the others kiss their wives after taking a sip from their glasses. He placed a kiss on Mabel's forehead and leaned into her ear.

"Merry Christmas, Mabel. You're my Christmas miracle."

Mabel giggled and lifted her head to stare at him. "Merry Christmas, Zach. You're my miracle too."

"Attention, please. I would like to say something to the house too, to add to the toast given," Brandon said, rising to his feet. "My vote of thanks also goes to Zach. It's a long story, but I would like to commend him also. You might look tough, but you're a sweet person, Zach. Thank you for your help with the ranch. Thank you for standing up for me. Thank you, Zach. I am so glad I get to work with a strong man like you. You stood up to those wranglers, and you put them in their place. You didn't have to do all of that, but I'm grateful that you did. I look forward to working with you. Cheers, Zach. And Merry Christmas."

"Thank you, Brandon. And thank you for the opportunity to work on your ranch," Zachary answered.

"You're welcome," Brandon answered. "Always."

"I must say this," Peter chimed in. "Mabel? Your intended isn't this uptight and quiet. He is a really fun person, and he is the kind of man that will go out of his way to ensure that you lack nothing. You should be proud of him."

"Oh, I am," Mabel answered. "He already confessed to me that it was all an act. He wanted to be the perfect gentleman but he only ended up acting awkward around me. Thankfully, we have resolved this, and he is now the Zach that I came here to marry."

"Good," Peter said and sighed in relief.

"Did he tell you that he used to have long and unkempt hair and he always wore a shoe with a hole in it?" Jamison asked.

"All right, she doesn't need to know all the details of who I was before she came into my life," Zachary said, attempting to cover Mabel's ears.

"Oh, yes, she does," Peter replied. "Did he also tell you that the reason he agreed to wear a suit to meet you, was because he thought it would make him look serious? He claimed he wanted to show you that he was not playing any games."

Mabel threw her head back, laughing. "Oh, Zach. I didn't know you were so nervous to meet me."

"I wasn't," he lied. "I just thought the suit was a good idea."

"It really wasn't," she answered, unable to control her laughter. "You looked like a banker from West Virginia."

"Bankers here dress exactly like that too," Drusilla said. "I saw him on his way to pick you up that day and I was confused myself. I thought he changed jobs."

"Laugh all you want," Zach said. "I looked good in that suit."

"Of course, you did," Mabel answered, placing a kiss on his cheek. "You looked wonderful in that suit. You just didn't look like a miner. But I know now, that you were only trying to impress me. I'm sorry I didn't compliment you."

"It's all right. I wanted to tell you that you looked really pretty in that orange gown but I found it difficult to speak."

Mabel smiled again and fell into his arms. "I know now. That's what matters."

"You both look really good together," Amy commented. "At one glance, a stranger would be able to tell that you're a couple."

"I feel good knowing that we'll be planning a wedding soon," Drusilla said. "And I agree with Amy. I think we all saw from the start that you both were a good match. It took Zach a while to come out of his shell, but he eventually did."

Zachary sat up and cleared his throat. "It would be dumb not to thank you all for your help with Mabel. Wyatt and Tillie, I am still very surprised that you both were quick to help me with no questions asked. Thank you for cleaning me up, and for the advice. I know I didn't heed them, but I'll make sure to do so now that Mabel and I are on the same page. Tillie, you told me to be myself. I should have listened. Thank you. Wyatt, you asked me not to be awkward, obviously, I didn't listen, but I know better now. I think the person I really shouldn't have listened to was Peter when he offered me that suit."

They all laughed at his statement.

"But then again, I have Peter to thank the most," Zachary continued. "He came to me when I was doubting myself. I know I didn't look my best two months ago, but the miners were being rude to me and they picked on me because of it. But you were the first person to sit down and talk to me casually about something so obvious that I failed to realize it. Not only did you talk to me about it, but you also helped. I'm grateful to you for it. I know that Mabel would have still accepted me, with my unkempt hair and all, but I will also remember how good I looked that very day. It was the first time I was dressed like that. I'll always remember it. I will grow my hair and my beard back, but neatly this time. I also have Carrie to thank, but she's in the kitchen, so I guess I'd thank her privately, later."

"You don't need to thank us, Zach," Peter said. "You'd do the same."

"I most definitely will," he answered. "I've never been a part of a family this big. I see now that Carrie doesn't just bring people together, she's creating a family of friends. People that look out for one another. I'm glad Mabel and I are part of this and I'm so happy that the days I spent stalking Carrie in the hope that she'd give me an audience paid off. This is by a mile, the best Christmas I've ever had."

"Oh, it's still too early in the day," Jamison said. "You should see how interesting it gets when we have hot cocoa in our hand and we surround the fireplace to talk about what we're grateful for."

"I look forward to it," Zachary said and sat back. He held Mabel in his arms again with a bright smile on his face.

"Oh, do you all remember that Christmas when Gloria came to Gray Rock?" Drusilla asked.

"When Steven called Eugene 'dad' for the first time?" Jamison asked.

"Yes. It was so sweet."

"I remember how we all cried," Gloria said. "Eugene cried the most."

"I will admit to that," Eugene chimed in. "It was the best day of my life. My own Christmas miracle. I will never forget it. Ever."

As they all shared stories of Christmas memories they were never going to forget, Zachary made a mental note to write to Peggy, telling her how blessed he felt to be part of something so simple, yet, so wholesome.

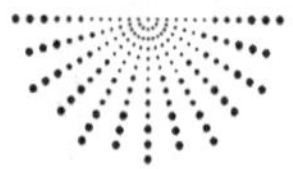

CHAPTER TWENTY-TWO

"Strong man, huh?"

It was almost time for lunch, but Mabel had suggested a stroll to Zachary. She had enjoyed the time they spent together the night before, laying in each other's arms, and talking about everything. Mabel's new favorite thing to do was to spend some alone time with Zachary, talking about his life and all the things he was most proud of.

"I might have threatened some horse wranglers that were making fun of Brandon," he said, swinging her arm as they walked. "That's why he calls me that."

"That's good. It's a good thing you stood up for him."

"Brandon's reaction to bullies is something that baffles and amazes me at the same time," he continued. "He just lets them say whatever they want and it never gets to him. He never shows any emotion or reaction to them. And I realized something. That his reaction is a threat too. I mean, if I were in their shoes and Brandon showed no reaction to the things I say to him, I would be taken aback. I would get tired of messing with him. I'd stop."

"You would. But not everyone thinks like you. Some people will see that as an opportunity to keep messing with him. But it doesn't matter. He has you by his side and I'm sure he has no worries anymore."

"I want you to feel the same, Mabel. I've dropped the act completely. I'm a tough man, and I can fight. I'm not afraid to throw a punch if anyone were to mess with you, or someone else that I care about. That's who I am, and it's who I will remain. So, I want you to be assured that you have nothing to fear."

"I won't go around making trouble, so you don't worry. You won't have to throw a punch because of me. But I know that I'm safe with you, you are my hidden hero. That's what matters to me. I've never felt this safe with anyone before. It came to me the first day I saw you in the center of the town. I just knew I'd found my safe place."

"Good. That's what I am to you, and I want to always be because I love you, and I will do anything for you. You have no idea how grateful I am that you came to Gray Rock to be with me."

Mabel felt her heart flutter. "You love me?"

"I do. I'm certain that I do, and I want us to get married as soon as possible. I want you to bear my last name and I want to spend the rest of my life with you."

Mabel stifled a smile. "Are you sure? I know I have been the one pushing for us to get married, but if you want to wait until you're comfortable, then I will wait with you. I'll get a job too, and I..."

"No, I don't want you to work," Zachary told her. "I will work for the both of us. And I'm sure, Mabel. I want to marry you. That's all I've wanted since the day I saw you."

"I'll do as you say. You know where I stand. Let's get married."

Zachary smiled sheepishly and pulled her into an embrace. "I'll let Carrie know."

"Zach?" she called him quietly.

"Thank you," she started. "I know I've said this to you before, but I feel like I need to thank you again. Thank you for responding to me. I was lost and I was about to accept a fate that would have ruined my life forever. But you sent for me, sent my fare and you said you looked forward to meeting me. Those words made me feel good. Like I was seen by someone."

"Well, if you're thanking me for that, then I guess I should thank you for picking up a newspaper."

Mabel raised her head. "Do you know that was just... I didn't plan to. I was at a diner, visiting Greta and I picked up a newspaper someone left on the table where I sat. I kept flipping and flipping until I got to the advert page. I looked through it, and was about to give up searching for an interesting one when I saw yours."

"I was the first person you wrote to?" Zachary smiled.

"Yes. I didn't think you'd reply at first. After sending the letter, I started to second-guess everything I wrote."

"Well, Carrie does this thing where she gives you options. She handed me two letters. I read yours first and I didn't read the second one. I was drawn to your words. You had written that you wanted a real man that will stand up for you no matter what. Someone that knew what he wanted. I felt I was that person, and the rest is history."

"You really didn't open the second letter?"

Zachary shook his head. "I didn't need to. Look at where we are now. Doesn't this feel right?"

"It does," she answered, grinning. "So, we both made the right choice for ourselves, and here we are. I see why Carrie has such a good track record. She's good at what she does."

"She is. Everyone in town knows. Most of the miners really want to go to her for help, but they're shy. I know some of them who can't bring themselves to ask for favors."

"Well, I'm glad that you did," Mabel said, falling into his arms again. "I love you, Zach. I can't wait to start this journey with you."

Zachary hugged her tightly and sighed. "Merry Christmas, Mabel."

Everything felt new. Like she had been reborn. Mabel had a new definition of love, trust, and of family. It wasn't a feeling she knew, but it was one she hoped would last for a lifetime. Who knew falling in love felt so good?

"Merry Christmas, Zach."

CHAPTER TWENTY-THREE

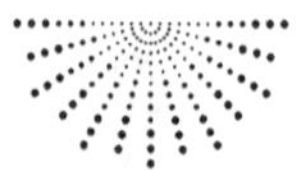

"I think you should just ask Carrie."

Olivia had told Brandon multiple times that she wasn't worried, but deep down, she was agitated. After she received a letter from her dearest friend back in Missouri, Olivia became restless. She didn't know what to do to help and it seemed as though Carrie was the only person to turn to.

"I don't know if I should burden her with this, Brandon," Olivia told him, taking a seat outside on the porch. "She has so much to do. Zachary and Mabel are getting married soon, and Carrie will take it upon herself to plan it. Amy just put to bed and she's helping the new mother with the child. Not to mention the line of men waiting to ask Carrie for help."

"Let Carrie be the judge of this. If she can't help, then we'll figure out a way to help your friend."

"Carrie has done a lot for us already. I'm not sure-"

"Your husband is right, Olivia," Carrie said, emerging from inside the house. "Let Carrie be the judge of... whatever this is. I wasn't eavesdropping. I only heard my name and I came outside. Now, tell me what it is."

"Oh, Carrie," Olivia said, burying her head in her hands. "I'm afraid I need your help."

Carrie glanced at Brandon before sitting by Olivia's side. "Tell me what the problem is. I'll make sure to do everything in my power to help."

Olivia took Brandon's hand and turned her attention to Carrie. "Do you recall why I came to Gray Rock in the first place?"

"Your father passed away and your cousin wanted to force you into a marriage with a vile man so he could take control of your father's properties and still keep an eye on you. I recall very clearly," she answered.

"That vile man's name is William Moore. He is a farmer in Missouri. I successfully made my way here to Gray Rock, and thankfully, I wasn't followed by my cousin. I have a life here. A good one. One I wouldn't trade for anything in the world. I recall how scared I was just thinking that I was going to be William's wife. But now, my friend, Felicity Soames is being forced to take my place. Now that I'm not there anymore to marry William, he has set his eyes on Felicity and he wants her to marry him. This man is used to getting what he wants by any means necessary. I'm afraid of what he might do to her."

"You want me to send for her?" Carrie asked. "I could match this friend of yours to one of the men here seeking a bride. She can even stay with me while we figure things out."

"I would be eternally grateful to you if you would do this for me," Olivia said, taking Carrie's hand into hers. "Please. I feel so bad for Felicity."

"Say no more. I'll write the letter and you can send it to her. Hopefully, it gets to her before she's forced into anything."

"There is one issue," Olivia pointed out, glancing at Carrie and then at Brandon. "Felicity might not be coming alone. You see, her cousin happened to get pregnant outside wedlock and she just put to bed. I've known

Felicity for years and she and Emily, her cousin are inseparable. If Felicity marries William, she'll never see Emily again. He won't let her be associated with her anymore. So, she can't leave her cousin behind. If she's coming to Gray Rock, she'll be coming with Emily and the baby. I'm sure of it."

"All right. We'll think of something. We always do. I'll write that letter, inviting them both to Gray Rock. Don't worry Olivia. Everything will eventually turn out fine. Don't worry too much." Carrie smiled, and it was a confident smile, she would sort this all out.

"Thank you so much, Carrie," Brandon said.

"Thank you, Carrie. You don't know the relief you have brought me. I know you're busy with the new baby and with Zachary's wedding preparations. Plus, it's Christmas and I'd hate to spoil the mood. But this is very important to me. Felicity deserves happiness, more than anyone. She is a good person and she was good to me. She helped me run from Missouri. I would really like to help her escape that life too."

"Someone needs to do something about this William Moore. Who does he think he is?" Carrie questioned.

"That man has ruined so many lives in our town. Two of his former wives passed away. One at childbirth, and one killed herself. I think there were two of them that ran away right before the wedding. He hits women for fun and no one sees the need to confront him because of his influence in the town."

"Well, sooner or later, it'll catch up with him," Carrie said. "Hopefully, our letter reaches Felicity and her cousin in time so they can get out of there."

"I'm sure she'll be elated that there's hope for her after all," Olivia said. "That's what she asked in the letter she sent to me. If there was hope here in Gray Rock for her to find happiness. I'll be happy to write to her, telling her that there is."

"I'll make sure of it," Carrie added. "Come now. Eat something. I've been watching you; you've barely had anything to eat all day long. I don't see why you were so worried about telling me. I bring people together. It's what I do. Of course, I'd be more than happy to help your friend."

Olivia could finally breathe, knowing that she had gotten Felicity some help. The image of William's repulsive face was still vivid in her mind. She wouldn't even wish the man on her worst enemy. In only a matter of weeks, Felicity was going to be there in Gray Rock. Olivia missed her, and she couldn't wait to welcome her dear friend to the town of great possibilities.

She just prayed that the letter would reach her in time.

CHAPTER TWENTY-FOUR

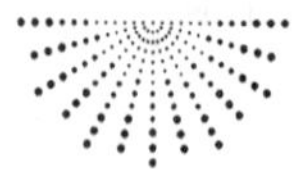

Carrie wanted to start a routine of taking a quiet stroll when she had successfully brought two people together. She did the same with Wyatt and Tillie, but unfortunately, she didn't stick to the tradition after she matched with Carl. Still, she was starting again. The stroll was needed for her to examine the match she had made so she could note the things she did right, and how she could improve on them.

When it came to Zachary and Mabel, she had not realized that Zachary had been holding back. It was only later, that she found out that he had decided to change who he was in a bid to impress Mabel. Carrie made a mental note to follow closely with the matches she made in the future. If they had not resolved the differences quickly, it might have become a serious stumbling block for them.

Thankfully, it ended well. They were both together now, happy and planning their wedding and their life. It was yet another success. Carrie smiled to herself, glad that there was an additional couple she had helped find themselves.

"Your track record is flawless."

The sound of a man's voice stopped Carrie in her tracks. She turned around and stared at a young, fairly tall man with a rounded waist who was standing by a tree.

"I've seen you around," Carrie said. "Are you a miner?"

"I am," he answered. The man was soft-spoken with round eyes.

"Are you looking for a match?" she asked, approaching him. "Is that why you complimented me."

"Oh, Mrs. Hill. You couldn't find me a match even if you tried."

"That sounds like a challenge."

"I'm not challenging you. I'm not asking you to find me a bride either. I just have a question for you. Do you think luck has anything to do with your track record? Or do you think you just happen to find people's soul mates from all over the country?"

"I'll bite," she said, standing in front of him. "Luck? I don't think so. We're talking about marriage. We're talking hundreds of advertisements, hundreds of correspondences. I go through each and every letter I receive for a possible match. I read them, find a common ground and I go with them. Sure, I've made mistakes, but who hasn't. In the end, everything turned out well. Matches are always made. People fall in love."

"I think you've just been lucky," he said.

There was something in the man's eyes. Something that could pass off as sadness. He wasn't trying to annoy her; he was merely speaking his truth. If Carrie was to guess, she would think that someone like him – who looked like the loneliest person in the world –was looking for a bride.

"Are you married?" Carrie asked him.

"No," he answered plainly.

"Do you want to get married?"

"Why are you asking? I told you; I'm not looking for a bride."

Carrie squinted her eyes. "Then why did you stop me?"

"I had a question."

"Did I answer your question?"

He shrugged his shoulders. "I don't think you were being honest."

"What's your name?" Carrie asked, crossing her arms.

"Abner Lange. I work with your son at the mine," he answered.

"Have you ever courted a woman? Ever? If I may ask."

Abner shifted his gaze and bit his lower lip. "I don't have to answer that."

"You asked me a question, and I answered. So, tell me this and I'll leave you alone. Have you ever courted anyone? Even if it was briefly?"

Abner clicked his tongue. "Sure. I can say I have."

"How many? How many women have you courted all your life?"

Abner crossed his arms defensively. "Three or four."

Carrie nodded. "My son courted once and he was able to get married to the love of his life. Now, I may not be able to speak for the others, but I can speak for my son and his wife, Drusilla. They are in love. It had nothing to do with luck. I just happened to send a letter to an old friend at the right time to be introduced to Drusilla, a jovial lady that was the direct opposite of my naïve son. I thought someone with her personality would bring Jamison out of his shell, and she did. Would you say Jamison has changed? The Jamison you knew two years ago, and the one you see now... is there a difference?"

Abner paused to think. "You could say that he looks happier."

"Exactly. Peter and Eugene, well... they didn't find their brides the way Jamison did. Peter had to try twice. Would you say 'luck' wasn't on his side, or it was just not meant to be?"

"Mrs. Hill, if you felt insulted by my question-"

"No, I wasn't insulted, Abner. I just want to make conversation with you," she said. "My point is, you might think you're unlucky having to try three or four times to find a bride and failing. But I'm telling you that it has nothing to do with luck. You've just not met someone that matches with you yet. You used the word 'soul mate'. Well, as much as I believe in love, I also believe that a person isn't tied to one other person. Love comes, and it goes. I was married once before. I was known as Mrs. McCord for over twenty-six years. Now, I'm Mrs. Hill and I'm in love with the sheriff. Would you say I made a mistake the first time? That my first husband wasn't my soul mate?"

Abner squinted his eyes. "So, what are you saying?"

"I'm saying, don't give up on love, Abner. It's a beautiful thing that you should embrace when it comes your way. You don't have to think that you're unlucky because it didn't work the first three times."

"I'm not giving up on anything. That wasn't the question I asked you. But you have answered my question, so I have nothing else to say."

"Deep down, you know I'm right."

Abner sighed. "What if the problem is me? What if I cannot make a woman fall in love with me? It's useless to try when I already know how it'll end."

"There's someone out there that will fall in love with you. With my help, of course."

"I don't need help," he said, staring at the ground. "It's useless. I think you're right. For you, it has nothing to do with luck. You make matches happen. You don't pick randomly. You select based on their similarities or differences. It's admirable, this thing that you're doing for people."

"I can do it for you too," Carrie said and shrugged her shoulders.

Abner scoffed, shaking his head. "You've been talking to me for a while now. If you were a lady that was interested in courting me, would you honestly agree to talk to me again?"

"Of course. I find you delightful."

"Don't patronize me, Mrs. Hill. I know my flaws, and I've accepted them."

"Good, that's a start," Carrie said, taking a step forward. "I can see it in your eyes, Abner. No matter how much you would like to deny it. I see it very clearly because I have seen it before. Now, you're a handsome man. You're calm, you don't like to raise your voice. You're charming. But you're also lonely. Very lonely. You don't think anyone would want to be with a man like you. But I think otherwise. Now, I'll ask you one more time, and I want you to be honest with me because I won't ask you again. Would you like me to find you a bride?"

Abner scanned the path and lowered his head for a second before lifting it to meet Carrie's gaze.

"Yes, ma'am. More than anything."

Carrie stretched her hand out to him and gestured for him to take it. "Stay in touch," she said, shaking his hand.

With that, she turned to leave. In a few weeks, two women were arriving in Gray Rock. That was two potential brides for Abner. Hopefully, one of them would find him as charming as Carrie did.

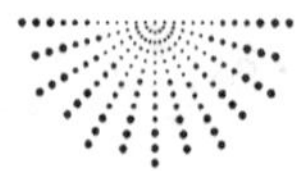

"Emily? Can you hear me? Emily, please say something."

Felicity felt a pang in her chest as she touched Emily's cold hands and stared into her still eyes. Emily was looking directly at her, but there were no emotions in her eyes, no movement, no feeling... nothing. She wasn't breathing anymore.

"Oh, no, Emily," Felicity sobbed, shaking. "Please don't do this to me. Don't die on me. I'm begging you. I need you; your child needs you. What are we going to do? It's Christmas."

With quivering lips, Felicity picked up the baby from the crib and placed her on the bed. "You can't leave your child like this. I don't know what to do. Please, don't leave us. Wake up."

Deep down, Felicity knew that her cousin was gone. There was no life in her eyes. They had seen it coming, but every time Emily tried to talk about her death, Felicity always shut her up because she didn't want to think about it. Now that Emily was gone, she had no idea how she was to proceed.

Ignoring all the voices in her head telling her to give up, Felicity stood up from the bed, placed a kiss on her cousin's forehead, and picked up the baby.

"I can't stay here," she whispered, scanning the small room. "We can't stay here, baby. It's not safe for us. We're in danger."

The last thing Emily wanted for her child was for her to be shipped off to an orphanage because there was no one to take care of her. Felicity wanted to take care of the baby herself but a man was preventing her from doing so. William Moore, the awful farmer who wanted to ruin her life by marrying her. William was unkind to women. The ones he forced to marry in the past had either ran away or passed away. He was a terrible man who did anything to get what he wanted.

Since Olivia had fled the town, his new target was now Felicity. He had vowed to send the baby to an orphanage if Emily happened to die. William Moore claimed that he would not take care of another man's baby, especially one born out of wedlock. Felicity had no intention of marrying the man, but she couldn't stay in the town either. If she kept resisting, she feared that William would put his hands on her and force her into marriage.

"It's Christmas," Felicity kept on repeating as she packed her bags. "I can't believe this is happening."

Her plan had been to run all along, except she had planned the escape with her cousin, Emily. She had hoped that Emily would get better after childbirth and that they would leave town together after Christmas. Felicity never imagined that she'd be running out of town on Christmas day.

There was hope in Colorado. At least she hoped so. Since Olivia had claimed that she found happiness in a small mining town, Felicity wondered if her own happiness was buried there in that town too. Thinking about it, she and Olivia were running from the same person, and they were going to meet soon, in the same place. Felicity held hope that her story would end up similar to Olivia's.

There was hope in Gray Rock. There had to be. For her sake, and for the baby.

If you missed book 1 The Miners Courageous Bride you can grab it here or read on for a fabulous bargain.

CHRISTMAS BRIDES AND SEASONAL WISHES PREVIEW

Amazing Box Set of sweet romances FREE with KU or just 0.99 for a limited time.

Bradley jolted awake, his heart pounding as a sudden screaming filled the room. It crushed his heart and made his head feel like it was about to explode. Dragging himself out of his sleep, Bradley rolled over and looked at the crib by his bed. His daughter was lying there, trying to chew on her blanket as she screamed, tears rolling down her chubby red cheeks.

Not again. This was the third time this week Charlotte had woken up in the middle of the night. Normally, she slept pretty well, but lately, she had been really struggling. Bradley had no idea what was wrong with her and it chewed up his insides hearing it. It made him feel inadequate. Whatever it was, it left Charlotte in a lot of pain, judging by the cries.

Sighing, Bradley rubbed his eyes and sat up, leaning over the side of the crib.

"What's the matter now, sweetie? Come here."

Charlotte clung to him as Bradley lifted her, cuddling her against his chest as he sat on the edge of the bed, rocking her gently while he stroked her head. For a moment, he was struck by how heavy his daughter was getting. It only seemed a moment ago that she was so light he was afraid of dropping her in case she broke into many pieces. She had been tiny, and she didn't wriggle as much. Bradley had stared at her for hours, wondering how he was a father to such a beautiful child.

If only Jacqueline was around to see her daughter grow. A pang of grief hit him, whenever he looked at Charlotte. His daughter was the spitting image of her mother, and Bradley felt the hollow sensation in his chest getting bigger each time. Jacqueline was supposed to be here, raising their child together. She shouldn't have been taken like that.

The pain of her death was getting easier to deal with, but not by much. Bradley had work and his daughter to focus on. Charlotte more than anything eased the pain. She needed his time, money, attention, and love, and Bradley had made himself a promise not to let his daughter go without. Caring for her prevented him from wallowing in his own self-pity.

She was still crying in his arms, now chewing on his fingers. Perhaps she was hungry. Putting her on the bed for a moment, Bradley tugged on his trousers, shrugging on a shirt but not buttoning it up. Charlotte whined more as he dressed, it quietened a little when he picked her up again.

"Come on, you. Let's go outside and have a walk around the garden."

Maybe some fresh air would help. It had worked wonders when Charlotte was a newborn and just wouldn't sleep, even after being nursed. Emma had suggested fresh air to help, and it had. So much so it had left Bradley feeling sleepy.

As he went downstairs and out into the garden, Bradley found himself having more admiration for mothers. They did most of the work when raising children. They had to nurse the baby, get up with them in the night and entertain them. They were the ones who made sure their children were safe, fed, and well. Fathers did get involved, but it seemed natural to pass it all onto the mother. Bradley had more respect for mothers who did this with all their children, especially when there were lots of them. He didn't think he could cope with more than one child right now. Charlotte was more than enough.

Especially when he was alone.

Jacqueline shouldn't have died. She should be here now, helping him and giving Charlotte the cuddles she needed from a mother. But fate had got in the way, and she had died moments after giving birth. Bradley had held her in his arms as she slipped away, torn between relief that his daughter was alive and distraught that his wife was gone. The days after her death were a complete blur. If it hadn't been for Emma, Molly, and his neighbors, he would have gone down a different route.

Nine months later and Bradley still missed her. He was getting used to being the one who got up during the night when Charlotte needed something, and he was used to being exhausted going to work, but it didn't stop him from missing his wife.

He could only hope that Jacqueline would be proud of him.

Bradley walked once around the garden, and Charlotte did calm down a bit. She was still whining and chewing on her fingers, but she wasn't as loud as before. At least she wouldn't disrupt the neighbors at this time of night. Hopefully, he could get her back inside and nobody would have noticed.

Too late. There were footsteps, and then a head popped over the wall, searching the darkness as she raised a candle over her head.

"Bradley?"

"Oh, hey, Emma." Bradley grimaced, adjusting his hold on his daughter. "Sorry, I didn't mean to wake you."

"It's fine. I was awake, anyway."

"You are such a liar, Emma, do you know that?"

"Sorry. I hear a baby crying and I'm up." Emma Hilton gave him a sympathetic look. "Is she still not sleeping through?"

"No. I don't know why, either."

"Poor you." Emma started to climb down. "Go on back inside. Give me five minutes and I'll be over."

"There's no..."

"Don't be silly. I'm happy to help. Now off you go."

Bradley wasn't about to argue. Nobody argued with Emma Hilton, and he had to admit that she was the perfect neighbor for him in this situation. As a midwife, Emma knew how to look after a baby, especially one in distress. She had been a Godsend since Charlotte's birth, even looking after her while Bradley went to work. He had protested about it, but Emma argued that someone needed to earn for his family, and she was happy to help. She had even taken the little one to her job to be there whenever she was needed. Bradley had tried to pay her for it, and she refused.

He did feel like he was taking advantage of her, but Emma never complained. Then again, Emma was the type who was no-nonsense. She just went on with life without batting an eyelid. It didn't matter what happened, she was still going strong.

Heading into the house, Bradley took Charlotte into the living room and checked her over. She didn't need a change of diaper, and Charlotte refused anything to eat.

She just kept chewing her hand, and her cheeks seemed to have gotten red.

Bradley felt at a loss. What was wrong?

There was a knock at the door, and then Emma came into the room, a shawl over her gown with her long graying hair trailing down her back. She was carrying a damp cloth.

"What's that for?"

"I suspect that Charlotte might be teething. Her teeth are coming through and they can be very painful. A baby doesn't know what's going on." Emma sat on the couch and handed the cloth to Charlotte. "Let's see what she does with this."

Charlotte gave the cloth a cursory look before taking it. Bradley watched as she started sucking on the cloth. Her whines eased off, and then she was sucking away in silence. Her cheeks were still red, but she didn't look as distressed.

"Well, that actually worked."

Emma chuckled. "You didn't think it would?"

"I don't know. I felt like I was going mad." Bradley rubbed at his ears. "I think my head's still got a ringing noise."

"That's normal. You'll be fine soon." Emma stroked Charlotte's hair. "She's going to be fine, although you might have some broken sleep for a while."

"You mean no more than usual?"

"Fair point. You might be lucky and she sleeps for longer this morning."

Bradley grunted.

"And knowing my luck, I'll end up missing the start of my shift. Then I'll get unhappy people using the stagecoach."

"You'll be up. Don't worry about it." Emma patted his shoulder. "If you think being a parent to one is bad enough, try getting woken up in the middle of the night because someone's gone into labor and they're in a panic. I don't think I've slept properly since I was younger than you."

"Does it get better?"

"Of course, it does."

Bradley yawned. He loved his daughter, but he could feel his sleep suffering. That wasn't fair on Charlotte if he was complaining about lack of sleep, but Bradley didn't really want to fall off the coach when he was working because he was falling asleep. He had done that when he was wide awake, and the fall hadn't been pleasant. It was not something he wanted to go through again.

"What I really need is someone who does this full-time instead of me asking the neighbors for help. I think I could afford for someone to come in, but at the same time, I feel like I'm failing Charlotte by doing it."

"You mean get a nanny?"

"Is that the word? I'm too tired to think right now."

Emma smiled. "Well, I think it's a good idea. You're not going to fail Charlotte. You're making sure she's got someone with their full attention on her. It'll be worth the money."

"The problem is, the nannies in Lubbock are already in employment, and I don't think they would have time to take on another child."

"Then I might be able to help."

Bradley frowned. "How so?" Emma smiled and sat back.

"I have three young ladies coming to Lubbock tomorrow. You're picking them up from the next town."

"Young ladies?" It took a moment for Bradley's mind to clear. "These are the ladies you've brought in to find husbands?"

"Yes."

Emma, as well as being a midwife and helping Bradley, still wanted to do something. She was always trying to help others and women were in short supply. So, she decided to become a matchmaker. Bradley had laughed when she first said it, but Emma was determined. At first, though, there hadn't been anyone interested in coming to Texas to marry someone they hadn't met before. But, now three women were coming? Bradley wasn't sure whether to be impressed with Emma's tenacity or sorry for the women to be put in a position where they had to travel across the country for love that might not be there.

"Anyway, one of them said in her letters that she's a nanny in Chicago, and she would be looking for work once she got here. You could hire her to look after Charlotte."

"Hire her?" Bradley mused. "Would I be able to afford her?"

"More than likely. You won't know until you ask. It will certainly help you feel less stressed about raising Charlotte."

"And does that mean more sleep?"

Emma chuckled.

"Cheeky. It won't hurt to ask her, although maybe wait until she gets into Lubbock. She probably won't want to be accosted so suddenly."

Bradley yawned again, trying to hide it behind his hand. Charlotte was far calmer, snuggled up against his side as she chewed on the wet cloth. It seemed to be helping.

"I'm surprised you're even suggesting someone else, seeing as you love spending time with Charlotte. You could be a nanny yourself."

"I'm all for cuddling babies, but even I need my sleep."

"And you called me cheeky."

"At my age, I'm allowed." Emma yawned and got to her feet. "Speaking of sleep, I'd better go back. Will you be all right now?"

"I should be. Thanks, Emma."

"Any time." Emma leaned over and kissed his cheek. "Don't fret, Bradley. Things will work out... eventually."

Bradley hoped so. He really hoped so.

Grab this amazing box set - 26 Christmas Brides and Seasonal Wishes for FREE with Kindle Unlimited

The Brides of Broken Bow

If you missed any of this series, all three books are now available.
Each book covers one couple and is a complete story.

God bless,

Indiana Wake

Indiana Wake was born in Denver, Colorado, where she learned to love the outdoors and horses. At the age of eleven, her parents moved to the United Kingdom to follow her father's career.

It was a strange and foreign new world, and it took a while for her to settle down. Her mom raised horses and Indiana soon learned to ride. She would often escape on horseback imagining she was back in the Wild West. As well as horses, Indiana escaped into fiction and dreamed of all the friends she had left behind.

From an early age, she loved stories. They were always sweet and clean and, more often than not, included horses, cowboys, and most importantly of all a happy ever after. As she got older, she would often be found making up her own stories and would tell them to anyone who would listen.

As she grew up, she continued to write, but marriage and a job stole some of her dreams. Then one day she was discussing with a friend at church, how hard it was to get sweet and clean fiction. Though very shy about her writing Indiana agreed to share one of her stories. That friend loved the story and suggested she publish it on kindle. Together they worked really hard, and the rest, as they say, is history.

Indiana has had multiple number-one bestsellers and now makes her living from her writing. She believes she was truly blessed to be given this opportunity and thanks each and every one of her readers for making her dream come true.